LAGANSIDE LIGHTS

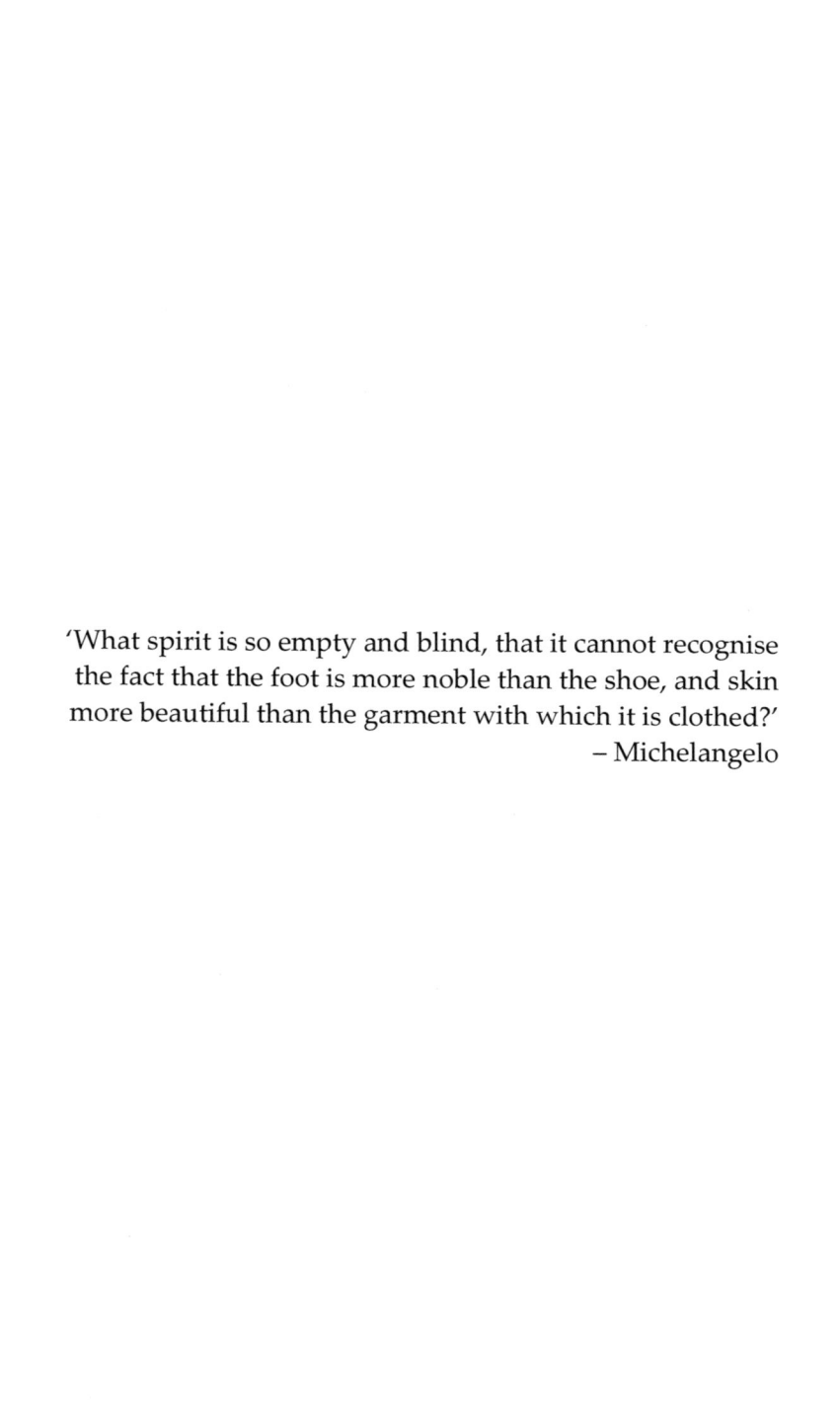

'What spirit is so empty and blind, that it cannot recognise the fact that the foot is more noble than the shoe, and skin more beautiful than the garment with which it is clothed?'
– Michelangelo

Rosemary Jenkinson

LAGANSIDE LIGHTS

Laganside Lights

is published on 10 April 2025 by

ARLEN HOUSE
42 Grange Abbey Road
Baldoyle
Dublin D13 A0F3
Ireland
Email: arlenhouse@gmail.com
www.arlenhouse.ie

ISBN 978–1–85132–335–7, paperback

International distribution:
SYRACUSE UNIVERSITY PRESS
621 Skytop Road, Suite 110
Syracuse
New York 13244–5290
USA
Email: supress@syr.edu
www.syracuseuniversitypress.syr.edu

© Rosemary Jenkinson, 2025

The moral right of the author has been asserted

Typesetting by Arlen House

Cover image by Patrick Fitzsimons

Contents

9   The Peacemaker

27   Bonjour Amour

48   The Book of Life

57   Laganside Lights

64   Going Zero

75   Homelands of the Tswana

98   Sexploits of a Rooftopper

109   The Whistleblower

123   Boglands

135   Waiting at Milltown

150   All About Erin

172   Brewboy East

183   *Acknowledgements*

184   *About the Author*

Laganside Lights

THE PEACEMAKER

The Castlereagh Hills lay ahead, their lush slopes brightening and darkening under the usual equivocation of sunshine and rainclouds. Shane turned right along the Castlereagh Road and parked outside a house at the top of a cul-de-sac. He remembered with a chuckle how his Ballymurphy mother used to call it a cool-de-sac as if it was the height of sophistication.

He tooted the horn and waited for Finn to come to the front door and hug her friend goodbye. Those moments afforded him a chance to observe her, dressed as she was in hippy flares and a Motörhead t-shirt in some sort of seventies fusion. Confusion, he thought to himself, though he had to admit she always looked cool for band practice. Her hair had a pink streak at the front and was pushed back at the sides to show her ear piercings in all their glory. She flung her guitar case into the back and jumped in beside him.

'Alright, Dad?'

'Sure thing, Stench.' He liked to tease her for her nickname, though what could you expect from a band called Stinky Girls. 'Who was that girl then? Bogging? Minging?'

'Yeah, right. No, her name's Classic Jill. She's named after this woman called Jill who wouldn't stop puking on the ferry. Now, if any of us throw up, we call it doing a Classic Jill.'

He guessed you had to be fifteen to find it sidesplittingly funny. He noticed how she kept playing compulsively with her rings, twisting them round and round, moving from one finger to another. Some of the rings were finely wrought; others were skull knuckledusters. Confused was the word that popped into his head again.

Once they were home, he carried his suitcase downstairs and phoned for a taxi. He could hear Finn playing her guitar up in her room. She was singing the old PJ Harvey song, 'Sheela-Na-Gig'. Her high voice vibrated, pulsed with a feminist rage that seemed too old for her years.

> Put money in your idol hole
> Put money in your idol hole
> Gonna wash that man right out of my hair
> Gonna wash that man right out of my hair

'That's me off now!' he shouted up to her, wondering if he should run up and exact a goodbye kiss, but decided against it. She was in her own world and would stay there till her mother came home.

At the airport he ignored Cafeteria City and headed straight to the bar.

'That's me on holiday now,' he said to himself, taking a long draught of beer. Well, on a work junket, he corrected himself, but it was always the same when he left home. His previous trips to Colombia, Somalia, Sudan, Syria or wherever had always been a chance to unwind. The paradox was that war zones were the places where he felt most at peace. A wry thought passed through his head that family life was harder than anything he'd gone through in the Troubles.

A recent recollection of Finn kept unsettling him. It was the day she'd got into his car wearing her steampunk sunglasses and black leather coat like she was about to fight the Matrix and had haltingly told him about a girl she liked from Queer-Straight Club at school. He hadn't known what to say.

His wife Deirdre at least seemed to get Finn. He sometimes heard the odd girlish giggle from the pair of them whenever he passed Finn's room. When he thought back to being fifteen himself, he'd been obsessed by war, and girls were just lumbers down the entry, a collision of tongue and lips, a wild grope, nothing more intimate than that. At fifty-eight he was an old dad, practically a grandad to her. He worried that her generation's genderfluidity had turned her into some cold avatar who couldn't love men, who despised them in some way and who by extension couldn't love her own father. He wanted to connect with her but couldn't help reading everything about her as a reproach.

Right on cue, his phone rang. It was Deirdre calling from work.

'You'll never guess who walked in this morning,' she said excitedly.

'Go on. Shock me.'

At first he wasn't sure he'd heard the name properly for the hubbub of a stag group in the bar.

'Olly McHughes,' Deirdre repeated.

'Oh, right,' he said, trying to stay calm. He'd almost expunged the name from memory. 'Did you…well, do the business on him?'

There was peevishness in her reply. 'If you mean did I give him a massage, I did. It's my job.'

'Oh, sure I know,' he said, the familiar appeasement scuttling into his words. 'I only meant it must have been awkward for you.'

'I can hardly hear you. Sounds like you're at some shindig already.'

'It's just departures. My flight's being called. Got to go,' he lied, to end the conversation.

He gulped down the rest of his pint, feeling the steadying force of it, then left the bar for the jostling mall, but the name Olly McHughes kept following him.

It was with him all the way to Warsaw. Excerpts from his teens kept shuttling back to him through the roar of the jet engines: how he and Olly used to pick up plastic bullets after a riot and sell them to American tourists in the pub for a fiver; how they went to London together to work on a building site only to miss the excitement of the Ballymurphy streets, the house raids, the swooping arrests and the street-corner whispers. It seemed fitting he'd been looking out to the Castlereagh Hills today where Olly had taken him on his first bombing mission.

At Modlin Airport, he finally got a grip of himself and began to concentrate on his journey.

The Kyiv conference room was full of government defence advisers. A smattering of army commanders sat cross-armed in their fatigues. It was the type of anonymous pastel hotel room where peace was discussed all over the world.

'Welcome, everyone,' Shane began. '*Laskavo prosymo.*'

From the low laughter he could tell he'd butchered his attempt at Ukrainian, but it seemed to have had a disarming effect on the audience. Or at least most of it.

'I've come here from Belfast to talk to you about peace and definitely not to lecture you on it – though I am lecturing literally,' he said, grinning, but the nuance of the joke was lost in translation. Tough audience, went the voice in his head. 'Thirty years ago in Belfast the last thing we wanted was reconciliation. Just like you feel now. We thought too much blood had passed under the bridge, but let me tell you, the most important thing of all is to keep the bridge open and, in the end, you'll cross that bridge to the other side.'

A commander dressed in khaki was eyeing him coldly, his head tilted in scepticism. He was bald and heavy-browed with a thick dark beard and wrinkles deep as trenches. The more Shane talked about negotiation, the more he felt a barrier push back against him. He suddenly wondered why he'd been invited. It seemed he'd made some terrible faux pas in coming here.

'The primary rule of negotiation,' he said, raising his voice to project confidence, 'is to pretend you're prepared to concede more to the opposition than you ever will. Lie if you have to. Do anything to get them in the room.'

The commander was tapping his thumb and forefinger against his lips. Shane interpreted it as a sign that the man couldn't stomach his message, and heard himself stumble over his words. He could see a waiter peep his head round the door to check if the talk had finished, so he wrapped up his conclusions in haste and left the lectern to lukewarm applause. Coffee and pastries were wheeled in. Normally, he was inundated with questions after his talks, but groups were chatting among themselves, avoiding him. To hide his embarrassment, he tucked into a cheese pancake. It was strangely sweet and crumbly on his tongue.

The commander came up beside him.

'You made bombs in the Troubles, right?'

'Yes. Quite a few improvised bombs. How did you know?'

'You think you'd be here if we didn't know? We want you to show us how you made them.'

Shane nearly spat out his coffee. 'But I came here to talk peace. That's what I do now. I haven't built a bomb in over thirty years.'

'Too bad,' shrugged the commander, leaving him.

'Interesting take,' a female official proffered half-heartedly while making a beeline for the trolley.

The next speaker was a Lithuanian whose message was passionately anti-negotiation. He pounded his fist on the lectern, touched his heart and slapped the back of one hand into the other to reinforce his points.

'No wonder our last speaker,' he said, 'was able to negotiate with the British. The British are generous supporters of Ukraine. The British are honourable. They aren't the Russians.'

Shane shrank in his chair. Everywhere he'd gone before, he'd been feted as the great peacemaker. He'd built a successful career from it over the past twenty years. This fall from grace was shocking and the worst thing was he had another two days of sitting in this conference room. At this rate he'd be booking a train back to Poland the next morning. The Lithuanian launched into a rousing peroration about the new Ukrainian counteroffensive. The commander was nodding in approval, sitting forward in his seat, even breaking into a smile. At one point, he caught Shane's eye, then quickly looked away.

Back in his hotel bathroom, Shane splashed water over his face. In the mirror he could see the flesh receding at the side of his temples, making his brow ridge seem sharper than before. It wasn't so long ago that his smile lines were at the corners of his eyes, but now they were spoking from his eyelids to his eyebrows, reminding him of weeds running wild. Still, as Deirdre often pointed out, he had a good head of hair on him and he'd stayed slim over the past years. It was only when he was away from home that he was able to look at himself properly. In a foreign country, he was foreign to himself somehow.

He swung his legs onto the bed, leaning back to check his phone. No calls from Deirdre as she knew better than to disturb him when he was abroad – 'in your own zone' she called it, whilst he called it 'in work mode'. He felt lonely but had already abandoned the idea of going home early when he still hadn't got over the journey to Kyiv.

He had a couple of hours before dinner, so he hopped over to the window to shut the blinds. The rumble of traffic filtered up from fifteen floors below. He had a sudden image of a missile smashing through his window and it occurred to him he should have asked for a lower floor. He chuckled to himself that the cheapest room these days in Ukraine was probably a penthouse suite.

He lay down and shut his eyes. He was exhausted, but the empty black canvas threw up a vision of Deirdre's hands slicked with oil kneading the knots in Olly's arms. He imagined how Olly's spine and neck would be rigid, every muscle and corpuscle contracted to its limit. Surely every single kill of Olly's – and there were many – must have written itself into his body. But the disturbing question was why Olly had gone to the trauma centre in the first place when he was bound to have known Deirdre worked there as a massage therapist.

No, he needed rest. He pushed the negative thoughts away, concentrating on the darkness of his eyelids, trying to draw sleep in, invoke it. Just as he was dropping off, a siren sounded from Shevchenko Boulevard, first low, then rising into hysteria. Low and rise, low and rise. An echoing haunt. He opened his eyes and sat up.

'Dear guests, attention please!' piped a female voice through the Tannoy in his room. 'The air raid warning is issued. Please seek shelter.'

He slid his feet into his shoes and hurried out onto the landing. A cleaner rummaging in a store closet for towels glanced over her shoulder at him in surprise. It was clear that Tannoy warnings were *de rigueur* for everyone but a paranoid foreigner. He was just about to return to his room, when he noticed the commander striding out of the door opposite.

'Want a drink in the bar?' the commander asked, stopping.

'More than anything,' said Shane with a grateful grin.

'I'm Volodymyr by the way.'

When Shane repeated the name, it sounded heavy on his tongue. On their way to the lift, a text came through. It was from Deirdre. It was one of the few times she'd contacted him in all his years of working abroad: *I saw bombs on the news. Are you ok?*

The timing made him wonder just for one second if she'd sensed him thinking about her.

The restaurant was packed with UN and Red Cross delegates conversing in a multitude of languages. Shane sat with Volodymyr at the bar, trying to ignore the adrenalined voices around them. The news was circulating that two cruise missiles had hit a suburb of Kyiv.

The bartender was polite but aloof. Holy fuck, Shane said to himself, there'd be more craic from a funeral director. Volodymyr, by contrast, was animated as he told Shane how he signed up to fight at the beginning of the war and was quickly promoted.

'My wife,' he said, showing Shane an image on his phone.

The woman was elegant and willowy as she stood next to her blond-haired daughter.

'Beautiful,' said Shane appreciatively.

'She was killed in the war.'

'Jesus, no.'

'Six months ago.' Volodymyr's face had tightened a fraction, but he seemed in control. 'It's war.'

'Doesn't matter. It's heartbreaking.'

'My daughter Dasha's my life now. She's in Poland with my parents.'

It struck Shane how wholesome Dasha looked. He couldn't help comparing her to Finn as he showed his own photos.

'Very nice,' nodded Volodymyr.

Shane, however, detected a hesitation. There was always artifice with Finn – the sparkly dew on her face, the kohl making a winged line at the corner of her eye like she was an Egyptian queen, the neon pink quiff, but it would be wrong to call her unwholesome. A lack of innocence was the real problem. Oh sure, every era had its own flaws – when he was a teenager, the church would have strung him up from the altar railings for impure thoughts – but all this queer-straight business taught at school was uncomfortable to him. Nowadays you were expected to think about your sexuality 24/7.

Volodymyr was flicking through photos from the grey zone. Some were of Russian soldiers; one soldier was lying in a porch, the boot blown off his left foot, his trousers scorched black. He was curled up on his side, embryo-like, the side of his skull a red midden, a few eggshell-thin shards of bone jutting out. Shane couldn't tear his eyes away, feeling a thud of pressure against his temporal bones, conjuring up the soldier's last seconds of pain.

'Am I shocking you?' asked Volodymyr.

'Yeah.'

'The Russians moved into our homes. So, why not throw them a housewarming party?' he smiled. 'We were only being considerate.'

Shane couldn't help laughing at the black humour. 'Ach, we were the same to the Brits. Sure it was only a wee bit of shoplifting whenever we blew up a shop.'

Volodymyr lifted up his phone defiantly, mock-showing it round the bar. 'I'd like everyone to see these photos. All these UN do-gooders saying they're impartial.'

'Not exactly flavour of the month myself today, was I?'

'What did you expect?' Volodymyr's face had turned ruddy with drink. 'Teach us, don't preach to us. Show us how you fought.'

Shane gulped down his beer. How could he explain that years ago he'd made a vow to Deirdre not to make any more bombs. Even as he formulated the words, he realised they weren't quite true as he'd needed precious little persuasion from Deirdre. Bombing had been a great tactic when he'd caused disruption to the Brits, but it was a different case once he'd hurt his first civilian. At that point, he'd fought hard to move himself out of the killing business and into IRA intelligence.

Already he was feeling the effects of the Chernihivske, used as he was to the weak Guinness at home. The commander drank incorrigibly like most soldiers Shane had met.

'Another?'

'I'm wiped,' said Shane, making his excuses. 'All yesterday's travel, today's talk.'

'But it's early.'

'If I don't go now, I'll never make it back to the conference.'

'Don't go tomorrow. I'll take you for a drive instead.' The commander was insistent. 'You need to see Ukraine before you leave.'

When Shane finally made it up to his floor, he was veering to the left. He could feel Volodymyr steer him towards his door. The landing appeared to be on a slope, but it was much more likely he was drunk than the architect had miscalculated the angles. He watched his hands fumble with his keycard. The signals from his brain didn't seem to compute with his body.

As soon as he lay down on his bed, it lifted and spun like he was joyriding some sort of mad flying machine. Nausea trickled onto his tongue and he knew he only had seconds to make it. He leapt up and charged, head-bowed, into the bathroom, diving onto his knees in front of the toilet. The beer promptly disgorged itself in three foul fountains.

'Jesus fuck,' he gasped, panting in time to his still-heaving stomach. He waited for it to settle and wiped his chin with shaky fingers. There was a kind of relief in knowing some of the poison was out of him to alleviate tomorrow's hangover. A few chunks of bright orange bile were floating in the toilet bowl and he flushed them away fast. He brushed his teeth, looking at his reflection through half-closed eyes. The mirror seemed too big, the light too mercilessly strong. He tottered back to his bed, laying his corrupted head on the white ironed pillow. He had the smell of half-digested beer in his nostrils, but it soon disappeared in the dark.

He kept drifting in and out of a feverish sleep to the sound of sirens without knowing if they were imaginary or real. Words were flitting around his head in strange connections, almost in a poem both meaningful and meaningless: Volodymyr, Floody Fear, Bloody Beer, Bloody Mary, Bloody Me, Bloody Hell, Blood, Hell, Me ... He tried to hone in on what they signified, but kept falling back into unconsciousness, interrupted by glimpses of Deirdre's hands on Olly's body, oiling him up, having sex, Deirdre's hands now on his own body, his hands on Olly's body, his neck, his forearms, his cock ... Finn's spidery splayed eyelashes rigid with mascara wheeled into his mind. And then out of nowhere, as he twisted and turned, the membrane between dream and memory began to melt away ...

A white plume streamed out of his mouth into the air, making him realise how hard he was breathing. There was something so holy and pure about the dawn. A white surplice seemed to be laid across the fields. He was walking down the winding road, the crunch of frost under his boots so loud he felt the whole countryside would hear it. His mother said she always recognised him by his walk. It frightened him that he was so identifiable.

He focussed in on the gate next to the hawthorn tree. He could just about make out Olly shuffling from foot to foot to keep warm.

'We better hurry,' said Olly as Shane climbed over the gate.

They both knew that the farmer, William Hogg, would be down at the byre half an hour after sunrise. Olly had catalogued his every move over months.

They strode across the field, grass crumping beneath them. The night was peeling back fast above the trees. He could make out the snow on the rocky hills, smooth as the pelt of a piebald pony. Above, a lone cloud was turning pink. He felt torn inside, anxious to get there, yet half-hoping Hogg was ill and wouldn't turn up. For days he'd been sick to his guts, not knowing if he could carry the mission through. The sun hit the tip of the hills. He kept checking for the bomb in his pocket. It was zipped tight, but he couldn't stop this feeling of foreboding that he'd lose it along with his courage. The orange light was moving metronomically down the white slopes.

They were at the gate leading to Hogg's byre when the dense hedgerow seemed to shiver.

'Hands in the air!' shouted a soldier ploughing through a gap in the bushes.

Another soldier cracked through the branches, pointing his machine gun at them.

Olly and Shane threw their hands up. English accents, noted Shane. SAS. His mind whirled with kaleidoscopic images of an army Land Rover, the shame of his parents, the headlines in the papers, the corridors of jail.

'Yess!' vaunted the first soldier, his teeth clenched in triumph as he turned to meet the smile of the other. He took his hand off the trigger to wave his fist in the air. 'Got the bastards!'

Shane didn't notice Olly reaching round to pull out the handgun, but he heard the deafening shot and saw the first of the soldiers go down from a bullet to the head, right through the beige beret, followed by the next.

'Jesus fuck,' muttered Shane.

The crows were wheeling like mad in the trees. His heart felt like it had been shot through his chest.

'Come on!' urged Olly, starting to run back across the field.

Shane followed, the freezing air sticking to his lungs, stinging them whilst his legs pumped along like there was no earthly feeling in them.

He woke up with a jerk as if he was falling, his face slicked with sweat. He raised his head and swore at himself for the drinking and for opening his mind to such a troubled night – God, he hadn't dreamt of those soldiers in years. The light on the blinds attested that morning had arrived. He lifted himself cautiously onto the side of his bed, his neck a little cricked from the plump hotel pillow. One fetid belch rose from his stomach and he rushed for the toilet, but after drinking some water, his innards overall felt settled. His tastebuds were screaming out for coffee; other than that, he felt surprisingly fresh. Above all, he felt purged.

He brushed his teeth vigorously, baring them in the bathroom mirror, then showered. He was good to go for the day, brand new as they say, he told himself. He wondered what Volodymyr had in store for him.

It was three hours' drive from the hotel, heading north past Chernihiv towards the Russian border. As Volodymyr's car approached a river, Shane spotted a destroyed bridge. An upside-down van nestled in the low water.

'Welcome to my village,' said Volodymyr, smiling.

A soldier, his gun low-slung on his hip like a rockstar with a guitar, waved them across a narrow bridge. A metallic burnt smell filled Shane's nostrils reminding him of the stale aftermath of his own bombs.

'When was this village last attacked?' he checked.

'Maybe yesterday. Maybe the day before. All the time, I don't keep track.'

Volodymyr turned down a lane and pulled up outside a small farmhouse. At first sight it was idyllic with narrow windows and white walls, but there was a ragged hole in the roof around which red tiles bristled like the bony plates on a prehistoric reptile, making Shane shiver. It could only have been caused by a missile.

'My home,' said Volodymyr.

The red tulip beds in the front garden were overrun with bull thistles, teasels and dandelions. The washing line was broken and had been tangled and spun by the spring wind into a noose.

'My wife was found lying here.' Volodymyr pointed to the grass beside a flowering apricot tree.

Shane felt a drilling in his chest and a rush of heat as the words sank in.

'Shot through the head,' continued Volodymyr. 'I was in Donetsk at the time, but the war crime investigators told me she'd been raped. She was bleeding inside when she died.'

'Oh sweet Jesus.'

He followed Volodymyr into the house. They crunched on a shingle of glass and tile.

'I haven't had time to fix things,' Volodymyr explained. 'This is only my second time back.'

'If I was you, I'd never have returned.'

A smashed computer keyboard had slid into a chasm in the living room parquet floor. Two of the scattered keys lay by Shane's feet. One said 'Home', the other said 'End'. Shane looked up at the ceiling to see that a hole had been covered with black plastic sheeting. Little bits of plaster were trembling above their heads.

They walked into Volodymyr's bedroom. It smelt of earth and damp. The coloured duvet was rumpled as if someone had just risen from bed. Shane tried to put the rape out of his mind, but sensed it had happened in this room. He could feel the lightest of brushes of Volodymyr's arm against his and his body made an involuntary spasm. His breath, he was sure, was in the exact same rhythm as Volodymyr's. He couldn't look at him for fear of meeting his eyes.

He was glad to escape the dark interior for the garden. It felt like rejoining the world after staring into the apocalypse. A blackbird with a vibrating tail was watching them and bees were jagging around in strange geometrical lines as if navigating a maze.

'My wife loved to work in the garden from morning to night. This was the place she loved.'

'I'm so sorry.'

They got back into the car and drove away. Volodymyr pointed out the fields that belonged to his farm. Fresh green crowns were sprouting from recently sown sunflowers. They passed a byre with a corrugated roof and Shane was struck by a sense of symmetry between past and present, thinking back to the Armagh byre where he'd been headed on that frosty morning. A month later, Olly had returned on his own and shot William Hogg in the head. Just an innocent farmer who happened to be a Protestant.

'I'm glad I brought you,' said Volodymyr. 'What were you ever going to learn about our war from that conference room?'

'True.'

'Now you can see what the Russians have done. Too much blood has passed under the bridge.'

There was only one thing to do on the journey back. To break his pledge. They passed dusty roads lined with wheat fields and a sky so vast and pale, it seemed to be a vellum on which every past act of his could be written. He told Volodymyr everything he knew about bombs, everything he knew about guerrilla warfare.

'One of my bombs injured a woman,' he confessed. 'I couldn't get over how I crippled her.'

Much later, they drank in the hotel bar till it closed. Shane's head was slowly building up tolerance for the local beer, though he still felt the tilt of it as they took the lift up to their floor. Something about the confines of the lift reminded him of standing next to Volodymyr in the farmhouse. He could smell Volodymyr's body and it was animal, a pungent matted fur mixed with a curious sweetness like meat with a wine *jus*.

'Why do you wear combats when you're off-duty?'

'Because war is everywhere,' came the terse answer.

It was the brevity of Volodymyr's responses that mesmerised him. It lent some sort of gnomic, philosophical heft to even the most banal of phrases.

'Goodnight then,' said Shane in the middle of the landing, but Volodymyr didn't move.

There was a heavy silence. Volodymyr's eyes were burning into him as they tried to convey their need.

Shane stumbled through the door with the magnitude of what was happening. They kissed and, as his hands ran over Volodymyr's back, Shane couldn't repress his sense of triumph. All these years of Deirdre touching male paramilitaries, massaging them, using her hands to heal them. It was like she'd cheated on him again and again, and Olly was the last straw. The intimacy she kept experiencing with these killers had been oppressing him for years.

Volodymyr was tearing off his clothes, revealing a dark streak of hair under his belly button, something wild beneath the khaki. His cock had sprung out from his boxers.

Look at me now, Finn, he cried out within. At last he was entering a world she'd understand, a world without strictures. 'Put money in your idol hole' rang through his head. He ran his hands up and down Volodymyr's arms, He thought of Olly's torso glistening, the oil swilling up through Deirdre's fingers. He'd known years ago from the way Olly had looked at Deirdre that he'd longed for her.

He watched Volodymyr suck his cock though narrowed cheeks and puckered lips, looking almost Mephistophelian with his reddened skin and black eyebrows beetling in concentration. He felt such compassion for this man. A quote passed through his head about how bullets don't only travel in distance but in time. It was the same with bombs. The reverberations continued within you forever.

He let go of everything and lay back on the pillow, carried away in the rocking pleasure. He heard himself cry out, anticipating the release right through to his bones and he wondered if Olly had felt healed at the trauma centre. He hoped so. A tear trickled from his left eye, taking him by surprise. He could see himself retreating, smaller and smaller as his train of memories pulled out of Armagh, the Shankill, Annadale, Cregagh, Craigantlet, the Castlereagh Hills ...

Bonjour Amour

It's taken me years to realise I never regret the men I've slept with; I only regret the ones I sent packing. When I was in my twenties and thirties, I was like some extremely strict immigration officer, letting a favoured few into my fertile land. I thoroughly enjoyed my capricious power at the time, but now in my fifties if one of those rejectees turned up at my door, I'd bring him up to bed in a flash.

Paris. A four-week residency. The offer came like a summer lightning bolt and I accepted immediately. I arrived on a sultry August evening at the Centre Culturel Irlandais – calling it the Irish Cultural Centre was just too prosaic. I took a lift to the third floor and trundled my suitcase to the end of a quiet creaky corridor. My room was monastic, having been part of a seminary, but its Georgian window and oak beams charmed. A room with a loo more than a room with a view, though it had an attractive enough outlook onto a leafy courtyard.

I met my first resident in the communal kitchen. Her name was Lucy and she was in Paris to research Lucia Joyce, so I privately renamed her Lucia. I always find PHD students strange for their weird niche interests, but it wasn't until breakfast that I met the full quota of oddities paying to stay here:

Oddity 1: Cillian, trad player and Irish language speaker – a professional Irishman if ever there was one – who looked like a lanky leprechaun. He had red shorts with knobbly kneecaps shaped like potatoes and the longest thinnest head imaginable. When he first greeted me with *'bonjour'*, I said 'bonjure' back to him with the strongest Ulster 'r' possible, just to let him know he couldn't pass in a million light years as French.

Oddity 2: The garrulous Cliona and her silent teenage son. Cliona was a music teacher from Dublin who was about to record herself playing the tin whistle in the chapel because of its 'marvellous' acoustics. I couldn't quite take her seriously as she wore blusher brighter than the plum jam we were consuming and a sparkly tiara as an alice band.

Breakfast itself was a spartan affair that probably hadn't changed from the eighteenth century. I helped myself to lukewarm coffee and hunks of baguette with the aforementioned plum jam.

'So, how long are you staying for?' Cliona asked.

'Four weeks.'

'Marvellous. You're so lucky,' she said in a tone suffused with envy and self pity.

For the first few days, I walked so much my feet felt like they'd been in a coffee grinder. I joined the tourist trail and trekked to Notre Dame along the cobbles of the green Seine and across to the funky Marais. I was overjoyed to be in Paris. Street singers kept belting out 'Je Ne Regrette Rien' on the bridges, but there was something I did regret ...

It was Charlie. He was the guy I'd been closest to marrying in my twenties. At forty, I'd emailed him when he was a plant biology professor in Edinburgh and he'd replied as breezily as if we were still a couple. I'd emailed back to say that if he was ever single in life to call me. He never did. I googled him last year and saw he had a wife and a grown-up daughter, but I'd always clung on to this dream of getting back together one day. Oh sure, I knew it was unlikely, but considering I was a rampant fraysexual, my five years with him was the equivalent of thirty for the average monogamist. Lying in my room one night, I remembered how Charlie had told me in his email that my novel was pride of place on his shelf and it was like I was still in his life. We still had some hold over each other.

In the light of morning, I banished these ramblings. It was as easy as wiping the sleep out of my eyes. Cliona was already down at breakfast, raving about everything being 'wonderful' and 'lovely' in a tired whingy voice.

'Check out the Jardin des Plantes,' she recommended. 'It's glorious.'

I decided to go for it. I didn't want to sit alone in my room. Since my arrival, the only company on my floor apart from Lucia was a beetle that had ensconced itself in the abandoned limes in the kitchen. I walked down to the courtyard and couldn't decide if the notes of the tin whistle emanating from the chapel were beautiful or high-pitched and cloying. Another writer-in-res called Claire was sitting at a table. Not that I'd ever met Claire, but I'd seen an arty photo on some website of her looking intense on a trapeze and I recognised her bobbed blond hair. She was typing in the bright sunshine – it was so hot you'd have thought her laptop would melt. I circled her for a bit but she didn't look up. I guessed she was luxuriating in this image of herself as *écrivain de plein air*. She must have been influenced by that famous shot of Hemingway tapping away on his typewriter under blue skies and, funnily enough, his plaque was just round the corner in Rue Mouffetard.

I strolled down to the Jardin des Plantes. A hot wind blew up from the metro grating and lifted up my blouse, revealing my midriff. A fleeting Marilyn Monroe moment, but no one was around to witness it. By the gates, I was passing a fountain with stone water-spewing serpents when I met the eyes of a dark-haired man.

'Bonjour, madame,' he said.

'Bonjour, monsieur,' I responded with a smile as I averted my eyes.

In the seconds after, I wondered why I'd broken his gaze. I seemed to be doing that a lot in my fifties. But it was stupid as the man had liked me, I was sure of it.

It was sweltering under the midday trees. Herbal scents floated on the wind. Since coming to France, I was more interested in my stomach than anything else. Give me a quiche over a cathedral any day. I was in the mood for falafel, so I headed out of the Jardin to a Turkish kebab shop. I took my falafel and garlic frites onto the shaded terrasse only to find myself terrorised.

'Bloody wasps,' I said, glancing at the man at the table next to me.

'They're African bees,' said the man with a smile. 'They like meat.'

'Well, they like falafel too.'

He told me he was from Chile and lived in an artists' residence at Gare de l'Est. By coincidence, he was also on his way to the Jardin des Plantes where he was monitoring certain trees throughout the seasons, writing haikus about them and taking photos.

'What's your name?' I asked.

'Felicio.'

'I'm Daisy.'

'Oh, I picked some daisies last week.'

'Well, you just picked up another Daisy today,' I was dying to say, but didn't as it seemed a bit crass. I loved his crisp curly grey hair and grey stubble.

'You're wearing a green t-shirt,' I pointed out.

'Yeah, I'm a half-plant half-breed,' he laughed.

He rhapsodised about Paris and it flashed through my mind to invite him then and there back to my room, but he had a languorous way about him and I didn't want to miss out on the frisson of the next date.

'Here, the writers of the past inspire me,' he was saying.

'Me too. I wake up to the same chapel bell as Victor Hugo did.'

'And current writers inspire me too.'

'I wish they inspired me,' I retorted, thinking of Claire. 'All the big characters of the past have been replaced by careerists. If the modern Hemingway was sitting with us now he'd probably be taking a fucking selfie with his beer instead of drinking it.'

'I know what you mean,' he chuckled. 'No more behemoths.'

'More like moths to the bright flame of Paris.'

'Look, I'd like to stay longer,' he said regretfully, lifting his rucksack, 'but the gardens are waiting.'

'Would you show me round some time?' I asked.

'I'd love to. What about Friday?'

He took my WhatsApp and shook my hand vigorously, moving his head towards mine as if debating which side of my face to kiss, before crinkling his eyes in a grin. He left without a kiss, but I could tell from the toothy broadness of his smile he really liked me.

On the way back I kept seeing the stencilled words *'Amour au Pouvoir'* on the pale pavements. Smoke was filtering out from the hashish lounges. The hot hands of the sun were stroking my bare arms when an icon came through on my WhatsApp from Felicio. It was of a broad leafy tree.

Over the following days, I had this image of Felicio caressing the huge laparotomy scar that stretched from my pubic hair to my belly button, healing it with his nurturing fingers. It seemed I was finding a worthy replacement for Charlie after all, someone in his mould. I shivered a little at the echoes – the exotic hot environs of the Jardin des Plantes had felt like stepping with Charlie into the university greenhouses.

Friday was even hotter. I waited a little nervously by the fountain of serpents and, as soon as Felicio arrived, we entered the Jardin together. He brought me to a giant rosewood, its trunk skirted with hexagonal stone seating.

'Let's sit here,' he said. 'Feel the strength of the tree at your back, holding you up. Isn't it great?'

'Yeah.'

'The king built this park to have sex with all his lovers behind the bushes.'

It crossed my mind that Felicio might pull me by the hand into the shrubbery, but instead he took me to the rose garden. The roses were past their best, but the smell was intoxicating.

'Did you know that roses are made from over two hundred chemicals?' he asked.

'No.'

'Beauty we think of as natural is so complex,' he said, smiling.

We passed impossibly bright flowerbeds and then strolled into the shade underneath the cedars. Felicio pointed up to the serpentine boughs high above us. The intricate awning of them. We stopped by a twisted, knarled acacia and it stuck me that the older the tree the more beautiful it was and it was true of us humans too with our bonier features and striated skin.

'Come here,' he told me excitedly, ushering me into a dell where a corkscrew hazel resided – *noisetier tortueux* better conveyed its masochistic writhings. Two dark branch knots at its base were staring out at me and I imagined being pulled into its arms. I put my finger through one curled twig like it was a wedding ring.

'You're not allowed to touch anything here,' said Felicio with a strictness that surprised me.

We moved on to more contorted trees, their snaking bodies slithering across the ground, freakish cherry trees spiralling out of the fat scrotal vases of their trunks, and woven-barked sequoias. Next, we headed into gardens celebrating the evolution of plant life, traversing back through eras to prehistoric pines and thick, unforgiving ferns. As usual, I had to touch them and this time he looked on indulgently.

'Sometimes in my life when I unearth plants, they tremble gently like this,' he said, cupping his hands as if they held two quivering breasts.

'Let's compare hands,' I said, holding up mine to meet his. His hand dwarfed mine in length and breadth and I felt the softness of his poet's skin. I badly wanted to have sex with him.

'Would you like to come and see where I stay?' I asked.

'Yes, that sounds perfect.' He was crinkling his eyes again at me.

Back at the Centre Culturel Irlandais, I brought Felicio into my room.

'Look at all the plants down in the courtyard,' I told him.

He headed straight for the open window. As he stood there, I seized my moment and laid my hand on his shoulder. He turned round to face me.

'Do you like me?' I asked.

'Yeah, I like you,' he said, confused, 'but I don't do that, no way.' He threw up his hands in dismay at my closeness.

'No, no, no.'

'It's fine. No problem. I just thought I'd try.'

I backed away from him and slowly opened the door like I was letting out a trapped, frightened bird.

'Ok,' he said, mollified.

I led him down to the courtyard. He'd recovered himself, but I on the other hand couldn't help feeling a downturn in my mouth, some kind of inner consternation pulling down my light chatter. He told me he'd been married but had got divorced at the age of forty. Ever since then, he'd been a poet nomad.

'It's wonderful out here,' he said, exhaling in the sunshine. 'The trees, the chapel.'

'I think you're sensuous in your mind,' I replied, trying to make sense of things, 'without being physically sensuous.'

Claire was sitting at her laptop, showing off her tan in a white sleeveless tennis dress. For once she looked up, curious.

'Could you take a photo of us?' Felicio asked her.

We stood together and he pulled me in tight to him, so tight he was squeezing the flesh above my hip like I belonged to him. Bizarrely, I almost felt manhandled. Just to cap things off, the stage Irishman Cillian entered stage left, plonked himself down on a deckchair and started playing the Irish pipes, his elbow flapping frantically like a chicken wing. I was in no mood for his haunting wails.

At the huge turquoise door of the centre, Felicio said goodbye and kissed me passionately on both cheeks.

'Next time, we'll go for a walk in a different garden,' he said. 'Will you send me some of your writing?'

When I went up to my room, I dissolved into tears. A strange word that, dissolved, but really I felt he had erased me. I cried not because of him exactly, though I liked him, but because I was older now and it wasn't easy to find someone open to sex. I realised I'd projected the image of a lover onto Felicio without reading the signs. And let's face it, as a lifelong reader I should have been good at it. He'd warned me not to touch the plants, so how could I have ever expected him to touch me? He was interested in plants, not bodies. To him, Paris was City of Light; to me, it was City of Love. And he was a haiku writer which meant he was one of life's minimalists. I should have seen that he was Mr Restrictive but I was too deep in my own fantasies and desires. It was probably a sign of my shallowness to associate the name Felicio with 'delicious'. From now on, I told myself to just enjoy Paris, forget about love.

In any case, I was too preoccupied to indulge in some pity party as I was getting love bites from a different source. The Parisian mosquitoes adored me – I wondered momentarily if they were imported African ones – and I went out to buy a mosquito plug. The instructions freaked me out – 'if you come in contact with the tablets, wash skin immediately, remove infected clothes'. It sounded like being in a nuclear contamination zone! Chernobyl in a plug.

I was happy to see some new artists arriving:

Artist 1: Aiveen, a conceptual musician. With her riot of dyed black hair and nocturnal work ethic, she reminded me of a vampire goth. She kept doing a pouting motion that would have been alluring when she was younger, but in her early forties only served to underscore the lines around her mouth. In certain lights, it was like a Singer sewing machine had savaged her lips.

Artist 2: Joe, a pretty-boy Australian artist who had an incredibly slow drawl that meant he hogged every conversation. He liked to expound at length on his liberal politics and, as a former chef, was unabashedly in Paris for the reason of food and fine dining. He was also here to work on a perfumery installation which struck me as a total French cliché.

Artist 3: Toto, a Swedish cellist in his thirties who was in an open marriage (sounded like bliss to me). In spite of being gay, he was irresistibly drawn to the company of women.

Our misfit group headed to expensive eateries on Joe's recommendation and drank wine while watching him guzzle platters of charcuterie and pâté we couldn't afford. As esteemed artists, we were invited to a fancy do at the Irish Embassy, but the finger food was so refined it wouldn't even cover your fingernail. Once, I met Irish tour guides and let them take me on an impromptu tour to a Champs Élysées café where they ordered bottles of thirty euro Brouilly all night. I was more than happy to follow in the footsteps of literary lushes like F. Scott Fitzgerald and Brendan Behan in Paris. Pourquoi pas? Sometimes I'd raid the fridges on my floor for discarded alcohol and sit out in the courtyard boozing with the artists for free. But it was best to be out in the bars watching the women swirl their rosé and breathe in the scent. They would cup their hands, moving them sensuously up and down their glasses. In the evenings, the light on the buildings took on the same shade of rosé before descending into darkness.

Every morning, I woke up to spit the vinous salival dregs out of my throat. Naturally, I never contacted Felicio again. I'd had enough of being led up the *jardin* path. Even though I'd given up on love, it was all around me. The familial relationships in Paris seemed almost sexual. On the train, I watched a mother wipe a crumb from her son's lips, and she practically had her finger in his mouth. In revenge he pretended to pull a hair from her chin. It was too intimate for words and being in Paris made me alert to every physicality. On the metro, I watched a man greet a woman by rocking her back and forth in his arms in delight.

One morning in early September, I turned fifty-three. Hilariously, to mark the occasion, it seemed I'd marked myself – I'd tossed and turned on my hot pillow in the night and woke up with the creases of it ironed in pink on my face. At breakfast it looked like I'd aged fifty years. The queen of goth Aiveen made a surprise appearance, looking unusually radiant.

'I haven't slept all night,' she told us.

'You look great on it,' I said.

I'd come to realise I was relatively sane compared to the other artists. They were all afflicted with depressive illnesses and neurotic sleeplessness and tortured themselves with their lack of achievement through the night. Some newly-arrived Erasmus students joined us in the canteen. They were cool and fresh-faced like the cast of a teen movie. I envied them their youth.

'Yes, it seriously bothers me,' I said to one girl who looked back at me, bemused.

She was wearing a tight t-shirt with a picture of a teddy bear and the somewhat sickening words, 'I'm sorry if this much cuteness bothers you … but I hope it does'.

I tried to rally the artists to come out and celebrate my birthday, but only Aiveen agreed. Joe wanted to stay and work in his studio.

'But we're in Paris!' I said by way of rebuke.

I couldn't blame him, though. He must have been tired of us pinching charcuterie off his plate.

On my corridor, more lightly-clad students had moved in and it was no longer a quiet haven. I looked down from my window at Claire in her mini dress slathered in suntan lotion like she was on a St Tropez beach. I lay down on my bed, relaxing in the heat and celebrated my birthday by indulging in a finger frolic. I was nearing orgasm, just bringing things to their conclusion when a viola and a violin began to play outside my door. The tune was 'Happy Birthday'.

I stumbled up, zipped up my jeans and opened the door, laughing. It was Aiveen and Toto giving me a birthday serenade. It was on my mind that they might guess what I'd been up to, but why would they? Then I realised that my belt was undone.

At seven o'clock that evening, I met Aiveen in the courtyard. She was wearing blood red trousers and a diaphanous black shirt that chokered her neck. I felt good walking out with such a beautiful woman. We strolled together into the varnished bar of Les Pipos. An ageing chanteuse in knee-high leather boots was slinking louchely down the narrow staircase with a mike in hand. It seemed we'd stepped into a Toulouse Lautrec painting – already I loved the sense of debauched seediness. The waiter offered us seats at the bar and my mood rose even higher when the chanteuse came round and flirted with us.

'Excuse me,' said a Frenchman, stretching across us to reclaim his half-drunk glass of wine. 'I was sitting here.'

'Sorry,' said Aiveen. 'The waiter said it was free, but you can have it back.'

She got up from her stool, but he waved her away, looking suitably sheepish for making an issue. After a few pleasantries, he said he had to go.

'Have a great evening, Richard Gere,' I said.

He stopped in his tracks. 'Richard Gere?'

'You look very like him.' He had the same longish white hair, tanned skin, dark eyes, black suit and confident manner.

A smile bloomed across his face. 'Believe it or not, I'm an actor.'

He told us he'd starred in some French films and dubbed most of the Hollywood movies. His name was Antoine Arsène. 'Arsène like arsenic,' he explained. 'Anyway, thank you for the compliment and have a wonderful night,' he added as he left.

Aiveen and I ordered another wine. All my senses were alive. I watched in fascination as a woman at a nearby table scissored her fingers along the stem of her glass. The faded chanteuse was singing 'Mon Truc En Plumes' less than impressively off a song sheet when I suddenly noticed Antoine's return.

'Excuse me,' he began, 'but I'm in the Corsican bar round the corner with my friend Jean-Luc. Would you like to join us?'

He looked at both of us as he said it. I knew he obviously preferred Aiveen as she was younger, but it sounded like an adventure. I could hardly wait to finish my wine.

The Corsican bar was packed. Jean-Luc was a thirty-five-year-old business analyst and it felt like we were on a double date. Antoine's eyes kept roving from Aiveen to me, everything was fluid, options in the air. I preferred Jean-Luc as he had dark hair and supple skin but he was more reserved than Antoine who was a force of nature. We four were squeezed in tight around a table.

'Why did you come back for us?' I asked Antoine.

'Because you said I was like Richard Gere. Wow.' His hand went to his heart. 'That is such a beautiful man.'

'I know. And doesn't Aiveen look a bit like Julia Roberts in *Pretty Woman*?'

'I do not look like a prostitute!' said Aiveen, laughing.

'You look amazing,' Jean-Luc assured her.

'And you look like Mia Farrow,' Antoine told me, his eyes shining.

Toto turned up and Antoine's brow furrowed. 'Another man?' he checked with me.

'Oh, don't worry, Toto's gay.'

'Great. Let's go to another bar then,' he said impulsively. 'It's run by a gay friend of mine.'

His hand slipped around mine to indicate he'd chosen me.

'It's a pretty good birthday so far,' I told him.

'It's your birthday?'

'Yeah, fifty-three today.'

'You don't look it. You look fantastic. And now it's time I told you I'm five years older than you.'

I acted duly surprised as I could tell from his sculpted eyebrows and moisturised skin he needed the affirmation more than I did.

In the street, I overheard him ask Jean-Luc, '*Est-ce que mon haleine sent le piment?*' and I chuckled quietly to myself. He dropped back to walk hand in hand with me.

'There are some French men who are *dragueurs*, you know the type, professional lover boys, but I'm not like that,' he promised.

I didn't care if he was or wasn't. Oh sure, I knew he was a roué – he was the womanising father in *Bonjour Tristesse* – but I felt exhilarated beside him. He stopped briefly at another bar to salute the owner. He seemed to know everyone.

'I was born on these streets,' he explained.

We pushed our way through a packed red-lit karaoke bar to order our drinks. The music was deafening, so we joined the crowd standing outside. I couldn't help noticing Toto deep in conversation with Aiveen, freezing Jean-Luc out.

'Are you sure he's gay?' asked Antoine.

Antoine clearly had an ulterior motive for bringing us to this particular bar. He pulled me into a small secreted side room that was under construction. There, we kissed.

'Don't go back tonight,' he murmured.

'Ok ... I'll go with you.'

I drank most of my beer down and told Aiveen I was leaving with Antoine.

'Happy birthday,' Aiveen said with a grin.

I checked my watch. It was twelve thirty. 'Ah, it's all over now.'

'No, it isn't. It's not a birthday but a birthnight, a birthweekend. It can go on for as long as you want it to.'

Antoine's apartment was in a nearby seventeenth-century building in a ravine-like street. The bright hall as we went in was enough to quell the headiness of the night, but he quickly dimmed it. We started to kiss on the sofa, then moved into the bedroom. A lamp in the shape of a rose quartz crystal gave off a soft bordello light. I shivered as he ran his fingers down the long mauve scar that stretched along my belly. His face kept circling mine as he plunged his tongue into my mouth. He continued to press his thigh hard between my legs.

'*J'ai envie de toi*,' he whispered

His penis was too soft to enter me, so he flicked away at it, his fingers simultaneously touching me. It was impressive multitasking, almost an act of magic. He came over me with a groan.

'Ah no, I drank too much,' he bemoaned. 'I wanted to be hard. What a bad lover I am to you.'

'Not at all. It was fun.'

'We'll do it again tomorrow. Tonight was the *avant-goût*.'

I privately thought that tonight wasn't so much the *avant-goût* but the *entrée* – or rather the non-*entrée*.

'I'll walk you home,' he added.

On the way, Antoine admitted to being a seducer in his youth, but in the last few years he'd lost confidence.

'I began to think no one would like me again. That's why I'm so happy I met you.'

When we reached the Centre Culturel Irlandais, a homeless man was lying crashed out by the hot air vent. He was wearing the thinnest of jackets and a clementine sat by his head – air con and a continental breakfast wasn't so bad at all. Even the homeless, it seemed, had a good time in Paris.

I arrived at breakfast the next morning with one minute to spare. I was decidedly bleary. An American academic was pontificating to some other overly literate gasbag about how his family name dated back to Catholic Elizabethan landowners. The breakfast bloviators kept tossing in titbits of Irish history to prove their learning. In contrast, Toto and I lowered the tone by talking about Manchán Magan's *Thirty-Two Words for Field* in Irish and trying to beat it with 'Thirty-Two Words for Vagina' in English.

'You two have sex on the brain,' commented a student.

'It's the only place I have it,' I automatically replied, before realising that after last night, it wasn't true.

A famous Irish writer was sitting across from me at the other refectory table. He had hair like a weevil's nest and a double chin bigger than Kingsley Amis's. It was always fascinating to observe the froglike dissolution of male writers. Once they'd ascended to the literary pantheon, they invariably let themselves go. I observed Claire slouch in and let out a delighted cry when she saw him, leaping into the seat opposite. I'd never seen her as animated at breakfast. The most she ever bestowed on the rest of us was a few grunts.

'It was a great night, wasn't it?' Toto said to me.

'Yeah. Antoine was a real French lover.'

'To be honest, I was surprised you fell for it.'

I didn't think it was remotely a case of falling for it; I recognised what Antoine was and I embraced it wholeheartedly. From what little I knew of him, he hadn't been fake when he'd romanced me. He was simply an actor and starred in a heightened film of his life. We writers were prone to the same overblown feelings. As far as I was concerned, Toto was just jealous. Perhaps he was more complex than I'd thought.

That afternoon, I met up with Antoine in his apartment for an espresso. He looked the business in his black jeans, grey suede loafers, and black and white arthouse t-shirt with a black suit jacket. His nails were impeccably white. I, on the other hand, didn't quite meet with his approval in the cold light of day.

'What colour is your hair?' he asked, lounging back on the sofa. 'Red?'

'I'd say ... strawberry.'

'I don't really love it,' he said, appraising me with pursed lips. 'I prefer dark hair. Don't you ever wear dresses?'

'No.'

'Men always love women in dresses. You know, it was hard for me last night with two women. I didn't know which of you to look at.'

I laughed inside at how I'd looked at Jean-Luc too.

His phone rang and I caught a glimpse of the name – Claire Amour. As he spoke to her, he stroked my hair in a possessive manner. The perfume he was wearing was overpowering. There was a rumble of thunder outside.

'Claire Amour,' I teased him when he'd finished his call. 'That can't be her real name.'

'Oh, don't worry, she's an ex,' he said, grinning.

I followed him into the bedroom. As we undressed, the bed was lit up by lightning. It was extremely theatrical and I wondered if he had a special effects team hidden in the wardrobe.

'*J'espère arriver à faire l'amour avec vous*,' he whispered into my ear. The expression didn't exactly fill me with confidence.

This time, I noticed that his body was incredibly soft for a man. I could almost have been sleeping with a young woman but for his unshaven face. I kept nuzzling into his neck to avoid his kisses scratching me.

'Sorry I didn't shave,' he said. 'I have *la peau douce et la barbe dure*, as they say.'

He was harder today and, as he thrust inside me, his forehead clashed against mine. He slowed, then speeded up, coming as the rain drummed hectically on the window.

'You did it, baby!' I exclaimed, feeling his elation.

'I tried going longer, but I couldn't,' he said, pulling away.

I hopped up for a pee. On the toilet door was a Willy Ronis photo of a naked woman washing at a sink. It was mesmerisingly erotic. When I walked out, Antoine was taking a shower with the door wide open and the shower curtain only half-pulled across. I put my clothes on, watching the white foam streaking down his inner thigh. I still desired him.

'I'd ask you out for a drink,' he said, joining me, 'but there's a problem ...' He gritted his teeth together. 'I don't get paid till Friday.'

'It's fine. I'll pay.'

I guessed in his life, women had paid for him a lot, including Claire Amour. I began to think of Richard Gere in *American Gigolo*. Antoine showed me a photo on the wall of himself and his attractive daughter.

'All her friends keep asking her if she likes older men,' he boasted. 'They think I'm her lover.'

Outside, it had turned cold after the rain. It was almost dark.

'I have a confession to make,' he said.

There was so much hesitancy I thought he was going to admit something terrible like a sexual disease.

'I'm not fifty-eight. The truth is I'm sixty-three.'

'Oh, but you don't look it.' I laid it on as he was so sensitive about his age. 'No way. You put the sex into sexagenarian.'

We were just ordering pints in the Piano Vache when Antoine overheard a young couple speaking English. The man was from Paris and had a curly black beard like a French poodle. He told us he'd met his English girlfriend in a bar.

'And how did you two meet?' he asked us.

'In Les Pipos. She was sitting in my chair,' explained Antoine, telling them our story.

It was clear the young couple viewed us as their older mirror image, but Antoine omitted the most important fact that we'd only met yesterday. He was already weaving an illusion for his audience, playacting the great lover.

'He's very *charmant*,' the man said to me, flashing a smile.

We left the bar. The rats were scuttling round the Panthéon.

'I wish you weren't going, but I hope I've given you some souvenirs of Paris,' said Antoine.

He meant memories and, to me, our memories together were far better than any tatty souvenir hanging on the wall. Images as bright as phosphenes would dance through my mind back in Belfast.

'I forgot to give you this,' he said, bringing out a frayed, flattened red rose from his pocket. 'I took it from a restaurant earlier.'

It felt like a perfect end to the evening, but it was strange how the accident happened, strange that the tranquillity had to shatter. We turned into Rue des Irlandais and just then, we spotted Aiveen and Joe arriving from the opposite direction.

'Hey, lovers!' Aiveen shouted out, waving.

As they crossed the road towards us, I stepped off the pavement to greet them. The lights of a car flashed round the corner – it was almost like watching a guided missile in slow motion. I leapt back to safety, feeling Antoine's hands grab at me, but the brakes shrieked to a stop and there was the slap of bone and flesh against concrete.

Antoine and I ran over. Aiveen sprang to her feet, rubbing her leg, hopping around, bruised and confused.

'Are you ok?' Antoine was asking.

Joe was still lying on the ground, clenched in pain in the headlights. 'I think my leg's broken,' he called out forlornly.

The young male driver was torrenting French at him, gesturing a mixture of guilt, innocence and disbelief. Antoine phoned for an ambulance.

It was only the next morning when I woke up that it dawned on me how close I'd been to injury. Joe's leg was fractured in two places. It was no minor incident.

It was bright outside and, as I rolled out of bed, I realised I'd missed breakfast. I went to the window and let the sun wash over me. With its afterglow in my eyes, with Victor Hugo's bell chiming in my ears, I opened my laptop and launched into a new email. I wrote everything in my heart to Charlie, telling him straight that though I'd loved him all my life, I had found a man, Antoine, and would find other men in the next years. I exulted in the fact I was going to go wild, live my second youth and have a million new experiences and I was alive, alive, alive. As soon as I had finished it, I deleted it.

At that moment, a hideous wail rose up from the courtyard. I looked down to see Cillian crouched over his Irish pipes again, his elbow waggling away like a lunatic's.

The Book of Life

After selling my house, I move into an apartment. It's just a rental for now, the living room part-furnished, almost Presbyterian in its plainness, and it will take me time to make it my own. Naturally, there are teething problems. The bath taps are as heavy as levers on a canal lock and in spite of the veneer of white paint on the walls, the history of grime is valiantly trying to break through, but it's a fresh start with a new view and I can see the Belfast sun playing hide and seek in the streets like a naughty child. The apartment is on the second floor and it's cheering to hear the amplified voices from other apartments float up to mine. Under my window, a blossomy branch of a rowan is offering up a bouquet to celebrate my arrival.

Once I've done my unpacking, the drawers and cupboards are bursting at the seams. I think of how Tom was always trying to free up more room in our house. I used to tease him that instead of man's quest into space, it was one man's quest *for* space. I try to dismiss all thoughts of him but it's approaching fast, this time of dusk the

French call *entre chien et loup*. Before the night has a chance to take on the black hairs of the wolf, I pull a book off my bedroom shelves and start reading.

'Is your name Void?' the driver asked us suspiciously, checking our bus tickets as we boarded in Paris.

'Er, yes,' said Tom as he always found agreement in a foreign country the safest option.

When we took our seats, we noticed the word 'void' written on our tickets and realized we'd been sold invalid ones. It was just sheer good luck we'd been allowed onto the bus as Mr and Mrs Void.

A very old English couple in felt hats were sitting across the aisle from us. With their curved spines and long noses they resembled fossilized seahorses. The woman had already annoyed her husband by hanging her handbag on the coat hook of the seat in front, its constant oscillation provoking him into detaching it. As soon as he was asleep, she bent her head obstinately forward like a tortoise and returned her bag to the hook, taking care not to disturb him. The feat promptly sent her to sleep.

The purr of the bus soon lulled Tom to sleep too. The lights on the ceiling and floor shone like a runway. All through the night we kept passing unknown cities, anonymous service stations and vast toll roads. Tom stirred a little and I saw the muscles in his neck swim and quiver when he swallowed, the thews in his arm inclining and valleying like dusky terrain. I couldn't settle. Exhaust smoke plumed out red and angry from the brake lights of cars. Some teenagers in the seats behind threw a crumpled note so that it landed in the centre of the old woman's hat, then tiptoed along to retrieve it. In the seat in front of me, a girl with a flat joyless English accent was rambling on to her travelling companion about how going ten days without sleep in Tibet was meant to make you really aware. I was certainly really aware of how irritating she was.

Giant European factories swept past, lit up like futuristic prison camps; big bulbous spheres on metallic legs with spiral railings. Silver funnels and domes webbed by an intricate interlace of ladders were pumping out illuminated clouds and weird sunrises.

As dawn lit the sky, we reached the pale ochre walls and red roofs of Prague. The elderly woman was trying to disengage her handbag from the hook. But it was stuck and she was in a desperate fluster, glancing sideways at her husband in case he'd wake up and see what she'd done. I wanted to help but it was fascinating to watch her struggle with all the 'will he, won't he' tension.

Finally, her husband opened his eyes, leant across and freed her bag. Then, as softly as the morning mist bathing Prague, he put his arm around her.

Tom yawned and stretched, smiling at the baroque facades and green bell towers. It gave me even more pleasure to watch his pleasure instead of watching Prague. His hair in that morning light was a fiery crusading copper, his face pale pink and delicately freckled like the interior of a foxglove. From that first second he loved Prague too, but above the city, the sky had vicious blond stripes of cloud like claw marks.

Over the following days, I leave my apartment to explore the local streets. I pass the back door of a Chinese takeaway where flames roar from a wok as though the chef is performing a magic trick. The very salt seems to be sweating out of the bricks, running in a line down the walls, just as the heat's melting the memories out of me. I stay outside for hours letting my skin go radished and red-raw, almost immolating myself in the sun.

One day, I wander into a Garden of Remembrance festooned with fake poppies. I sit down for a rest on the bench but can't rid myself of the impression that house blinds are twitching. The community is adamant about the sanctity of such gardens. Perhaps there's a written edict reserving them for the families of Troubles victims, but I want to tell them I can't stop remembering either. On a gable wall is the faded ghost of a white stenciled stout ad that must be sixty years old and I wonder if I wear Tom on my skin too. As soon as I think this, I head straight to a secondhand bookshop, breathing in the musty smell of escape and remedy. Books over the past few months have been my saviour and I rummage through the shelves, picking out the Penguin Classics and leaving with two huge bags of them.

It's the lazy mazy lengthening nights that are most difficult, from the moment the sun begins its runny egg slide down the sky. Instead of letting my mind marinate, I go out for drinks with friends in the Cathedral Quarter. Night creeps early into the narrow entries, making everyone beautiful in its shadows but when I return home, all sleep is gone from me and the moon shines through my blinds with a phosphorescent white, my heart shunting against my ribcage with thuds I'm convinced can be heard by my neighbours.

So I stick to my self-medication and start buying more and more books online and every afternoon comes the comforting whump of packages landing on my hallway floor. Each book represents a blessed four or five hours of pain relief and I read of murders, affairs, heists, ghosts and road trips, looking through the lines for guidance, consolation or sweet oblivion, but there's no story that can compare to my loss even though I'm feasting like a hungry xylophage on the freshly turned leaves, consuming more and more words. At night when I sleep I'm enveloped in their covers, lying there as if under the slates of a roof, protected from the elements, but they still can't protect my mind and I shiver like a dream-laden puppy with visions of the way the sinew on his hands used to ripple up and down when he touched me.

Everything appears to be dissolving. White powder stirred through a glass of water. Looking out the window I can see the balloons from a child's party tied to a gate, shrinking like gourds. I'm shrinking myself as I barely have time to eat between books. I might boil a few eggs in a pan and watch them roll round like possessed souls in need of exorcism. Or cook up a few lentils and beans and drain them in a sieve, staring into it as though panning for gold.

There was a Faust story from Prague that Tom and I loved. A penniless student who couldn't afford rent moved into Faust's old house which had been lying empty for years. The student laughed at the thought of ghosts or evil spirits although he found it wonderful that every morning there was a new silver coin lying in a black, polished bowl for him. He lived the high life, partying with his friends, wearing fine clothes, but soon the single coin wasn't enough to satisfy his ambitions. One night, he decided to turn to magic and blew the dust off one of Faust's old spell books, the white particles flying up into a ghostly warning. Undeterred, he opened the book and started to read out an incantation.

Just like Faust, the devil carried him off through the ceiling. I remember telling Tom at the time that it wasn't the book that was the student's downfall but the desire in his heart.

Summer moves into July, not that you'd even know apart from the heat prickling your skin and the sight of fecund red-hot pokers under pink pearly clouds. Every room in my apartment is now full of books and I read them insatiably, looking for echoes of what happened with Tom, for small morsels of hope, for advice on beginning my life anew. I scribble fragments of ideas into a notebook until a small glob of sticky ink starts to seep from the top of my biro which makes me think of a vein bleeding black blood.

One day, my phone rings and I can't find it since it's submerged under all the piles of books. A few times the doorbell rings, but I no longer answer. To help remind myself I'm still part of the world, I drag myself to the window and look out to see a cat languorously reclining on a sill like it's touting for business in an Amsterdam brothel. A wild lupin growing on a mossy wall reassures me of a better future.

I remember how Tom used to borrow books from friends like a smoker borrows a light, without ever returning them, and I breathe in the old tattered copies he's touched and imagine the smell of his skin on them. They're the only things I've kept of him apart from the photos and it comforts me to know my eyes and mind are following the same paths he explored, ascending Nabokovian heights, touring Kerouac's wide roads and plunging into Gogol's depths.

On our second evening in Prague, Tom and I walked down Wenceslas Square. Tourists knocked into us blindly, looking around for hamburgers or an amazing piece of architecture. They reminded us of a herd that would trample on its own young. At the bottom of the square, we stopped and watched a puppet show. The puppet master's hand was as twisted as an old witch's with the effort of making one of his creations moonwalk and Tom laughed beside me in that explosive way of his, like a horse's bolt.

We weaved through alleys to join the crowds watching the Astronomical Clock with its saints and skeletons striking time. Then, we bought some hot wine from a kiosk that advertised it in an amusing malapropism as 'Hot Vein' and as night fell, we took in the luminescent graffiti and electric blue flashes of trams. We strolled through the markets, past stalls of lace, paintings and metalwork. One of the ironsmiths was shrouded in a big blast of Mephistophelian smoke, his poker-tip eyes glittering. Prague was such a watchful city, the faces of its founders, stone saints and bronze communists commemorated in the walls. But we, no, we were not watchful enough ourselves.

'So, Mrs Void, is it time to go back to the hotel?' Tom asked me.

'Yeah, let's go, Mr Void,' I agreed with a laugh.

It was on our way back that it happened. Tom stepped onto a cobbled road without seeing the car, full of young Czechs on a night out, hurtling towards him. One step, that was all it took for him to leave me. One step. He lay on the cobbles, his limbs shivering, caught in one last dream while I held his hand.

It took long days to arrange the repatriation. When I finally left Prague in a taxi, it rolled past Wenceslas Square and I saw the puppet theatre lying empty, bare strings just hanging.

One book leads to another to another and I'm afraid to stop in case I'm left with night food for the imagination to later gnaw inside me like acidic fruit. Reading becomes a soporific act, casting a healing spell on me, but I'm starting to accept that no experience is identical to mine and my longing for Tom can't be replicated in fiction. There's no secret knowledge to be divined except that the temporal cannot be halted or changed.

Sometimes I hear voices from the other apartments but it's clear they belong to another story. They only exist to make me aware of myself in the way that a set of stairs exists to make me aware of my own body. I'm so inside myself, all I can do to escape my thoughts is immerse my mind in the written words of others.

Some weeks or months later, I look up from my page, aware of the darkness, wondering if it's winter yet, and realise my window sill's piled high with books leaving only a small chink of light at the top. For one second, I can't understand how I've let things get out of control. I get out of bed and try to leave my room but the door is blocked with books. I pull and pull at the handle, but it won't budge and a scream is funnelling up through my throat. Oh my God! I've walled myself in like an anchorite and I've no idea how long I've been lying here reading in this weird hermetic fugue. My lips are parched and my eyes are hazed but they slowly focus on the book I'm clutching. The orange cover is embellished with a black cross and black letters, and nestling in the armpit of the cross is the tiniest orange and black ladybird, seeking asylum in its colours. I blow on it till it opens its wings to take flight and, once it flies free, I clamber over to the window and wrench it open, throwing out the book. It falls like a broken-necked bird onto the pavement. I hurl more and more books out until light streams into the room – my pantheon to the gods of literature is being torn down brick by brick by brick, book by book by book. Now that space is freed up, I go back and pull hard at the door, pull, pull, pull and the books fall like a tumbledown wall, blowing up a dust storm of paper motes that nearly chokes me, but I manage to squeeze out through a gap into the hall, my feet sliding on the smooth slippery surface of book covers and I slither out headfirst as if from the womb.

And now I'm running down the stairs of the apartment block and out into the street and I can feel my heart rocket-launch into the sky because my mind is free of memories and I'm ready to live. I'm ok, Tom, I shout to the world and I don't care who hears me. Above me the sky swirls as if cloud has been shaped by a palette knife, and a freshness whirls down, making it a beautiful day for breathing, but down here I'm grounded, back amongst the living, and, as if to prove it, a passing teenager spits his honey-catarrh on the pavement. The rowan berries are the shade of bright saffron while the trees around me are as raggedy and tremulous as a witch's robe and I walk into autumn, knowing I'm cured.

Laganside Lights

Life goes so fast. I'd always acted like I'd won a hundred years of youth on the lottery and was never going to get old, but time sneaks up on you. One minute you're talking about contraception and pregnancy scares and the next it's HRT and the best brand of lube. Some of my friends were trying to rejuvenate themselves by buying new cars and houses, but personally I'd rather have a new vulva than a Volvo. One friend bought a book, *How Not to Age*, which was so long you'd have aged six months by the time you read it. Anyway, a few days ago I was in the kitchen when my washing machine was in the middle of its climax, lost in its thrice-weekly shuddering ecstasy, and it made me realise that even inanimate objects have a better sex life than I do. It was time to take the bit between my teeth (innuendo alert) and get back to dating.

That's not to say I was entirely alone in life. Six months ago, I'd met up for a drink with the new editor of the *Belfast Telegraph*. It was supposed to be a 'getting to know you' drink only it ended up a 'getting to know your body' drink which was not what I had in mind at all. There were so few journalistic outlets in Belfast it was foolish to get entangled with an editor, but the problem was I liked Will. He was a bearded, divorced Corkonian with a mischievous grin and anti-establishment spirit, and at forty-four he was six years younger than me. Our first meeting, he asked me to think of a theme to write about, but because of his southern accent I thought he said 'team' and goofily told him the people I'd like to work with. Falling about laughing led naturally to falling into bed.

'I'd better tell you now, Christine,' he said as we lay in bed afterwards. 'I'm not in the place where I want a relationship.'

'Fine by me,' I agreed. 'We'll keep this as a one-off.'

A couple of months later, after I'd pitched him some books and plays I wanted to review, he suggested meeting up again. We met in the Duke of York, a bar I used to love until it transformed into an Irish pub theme park with wall-to-wall Guinness mirrors, a narcissist's paradise. Fortunately, Will didn't stare into them too much.

'So, I read your pitches and here's what I propose,' he said. 'I love what you've written so far for me and I'm launching a new-look features section, so I'd like to offer you the position of features editor. Would you be interested at all?'

I couldn't believe it – my first regular wage in three years of being a freelancer, of hustling, bustling and muscling in. He told me the salary and I accepted on the spot.

He bought us another round to celebrate as some tourists gatecrashed our table. One of the Germans was so big he could hardly fit onto the stool and perched perilously on one arse cheek like some giant gnome on a toadstool, pressing me closer into Will. I blamed the German for our propinquity, though the pints didn't help either.

It was inevitable that the celebrations ended up back in my bedroom. I loved how Will's breathing deepened and elongated as he watched me undress. I also appreciated how he liked using lube. Some men, in my experience, took lube as a personal affront, as if it meant they weren't attractive enough to get us women flowing.

'I'm bursting,' he muttered into my ear, his voice thick with desire. 'I've two loads for you.'

Two loads! What was I, a washing machine? But I let it go as it was only an attempt, if misguided, to be sexy. Afterwards as we lay side-by-side, he asked, 'What happened to the one-off?'

'Ok, it's a two-off.'

'Or maybe an on-off.'

'Is this how you normally seal a deal with an employee?'

Beneath the laughter I felt uncomfortable. The power dynamic was all wrong. He was now my boss and I needed to keep him on side. If we got into a relationship that fell apart, I stood to lose everything. I couldn't face going back to journalistic grifting. My rented house was crumbling and my neighbour had warned me my yard wall might fall down on top of him. The last time my kitchen had been redecorated was by the damp. The heating was so ancient I had to go out to the boiler to switch it on. Perhaps it could be designated 'a period feature' but I doubted it and I kept tramping the moss from the yard into the kitchen which, to airbrush the truth, gave my house a 'charmingly rustic aspect'. As for my orgasmic washing machine, the drum was like a cheese grater and my clothes came out with more holes than a Gorgonzola.

I told myself to keep my distance from Will. The next night I went to review *Little Women* for him at the Lyric. The production was great but it troubled me to see a play where everyone gets married except for the sole woman who is a total monster. I wondered if one of the main reasons I wanted to go out with Will was because I didn't want to be perceived at fifty as some dry-to-the-bone loveless Aunt March. But I also knew there was a need inside me. It wasn't just Will's hard body I wanted, it was the softness of the aftermath, the friendship. Even though I might have lusted after guys younger than Will, I didn't honestly like young guys in bed as they invariably hoisted my legs over their shoulders or bent me into impossible positions like I was twenty. If I'd wanted to do yoga, I'd have gone to a frigging class.

Funnily enough, I'd been thinking for a while of Facebook Dating, but I just wasn't into digital. Besides, I was tired of shits that pass in the night. I also found it a bit off-putting that Facebook kept sending me an image of two women flirting. It seemed I was releasing some sort of lesbian algorithmic vibe. Perhaps it was down to me liking posts about women writers or, more worryingly, it was my profile pic. I decided to swap it for one in which my hair was fluffier and my chin reclined on the back of my hand, but Facebook was still convinced I was gay. It got me thinking about the time I went to this interactive theatre show and was asked by the actor to kiss my female friend. I actually tried to, but my friend rudely shouted no and turned her head away. It seemed that lesbianic love had never really worked out for me.

In the meantime, I wrote features galore about plays, novels, art exhibitions, hot actors and controversial Troubles poets. Will let me loose on whatever I wanted and I milked my freedom to the hilt. A couple of times he asked to meet up, but I always made my excuses, saying I had covid or was away. It was flaky of me, but the last thing I wanted was to feel I should pay him in kind. And anyway, relationships weren't everything, as my friends with settled partners seemed to be even less settled than me.

They were all buying shares in a French château in some crazy attempt at projecting success in their lives.

Before Christmas, Will contacted me again as he wanted to discuss feature ideas for the impending year. It was clearly work-oriented and this time I couldn't get out of it.

The following evening in the Duke of York, I arrived to him sitting at a table, a pint waiting for me. After our hellos, he handed me a bottle of wine and a Christmas card. When I opened the card, it said 'Happy Christmas, from Will'. I was kind of surprised there was no 'love Will' or 'x', but glad in a way. It meant we'd morphed from being lovers back to a business relationship.

'I'm not going to ask you for themes or teams again,' he said, grinning, 'but I meant to tell you a community leader is threatening to sue us over that Troubles poem you featured.'

I wasn't shocked. This country was still wildly oversensitive over its war-torn past.

'Sorry about that. I'll go easy for a bit with a few nice pastoral poems.'

'No, work away,' he said. 'They've no chance of getting a penny out of us. Let's shake things up instead.'

As he drank, the top of his cheeks began to blush like the alcohol had slapped him. I found it boyishly appealing, but wondered if I was making him nervous. After our pints, we walked to his car. I felt the tension as he drove over to my part of town. The moment was not so much pregnant with possibility as in full-on birth mode. I kept thinking about the times we'd spent in bed and sensed the vitality of his body next to me. At the same time, I told myself I had a great job and not to jeopardise it. We crossed the Albert Bridge and, below us, the lights spun and pulsed hectically on the Lagan, black waves running through them like ripples through fluttering flags. We turned into the shipyard streets.

'Maybe we can meet again in the new year,' he said, the engine still running as we sat outside my door.

'Or ...' I had to say something. 'You could come in now.'

'Oh, ok.'

In my bedroom, he slid down my body and used his hands to lift up my buttocks as if raising a goddess onto a plinth. He said I tasted delicious. When I sat on top of him, I could see his pink balls swell back and forth beneath like a heart beating for me. After he came, he breathed out cool sensuous pools of air onto my chest, then fell back onto the bed. I wrapped my leg across his body to feel the heat of it and ran the tips of my fingers back and forth through his chest hair while he swirled his fingernails around my shoulder making ovals and circles and figures of eight like he was drawing his pleasure onto my skin.

Later, his legs must have still been shaking as he stumbled down the stairs. When I walked him out into the hall, he asked, his forehead crumpled, 'Is the sex ok?'

'You mean ... with my body?'

'No, no. I meant with it being casual.'

'Oh, it's fine. I'm a casual sort of person myself,' I reassured him, wondering why I always had to pretend to be cool.

We kissed and he was just about to leave when I told him to wait. I hurried into the living room to write him a Christmas card.

'Don't worry about it,' he said, but I scribbled my usual wordplay of 'Merry Christinemas!' to make him smile, and added two kisses underneath.

Waving him off in the hallway, I noticed a paper ball lampshade in a window opposite, shining like a moon in a dark blue sky. A minute later, he was tapping on my door again. I opened it, my heart thumping at the notion he was about to tell me he loved me.

'Sorry,' he said, retrieving his phone from my living room. 'Head like a sieve.'

He was always so dazed and forgetful after sex. Almost drained by it. Maybe dazzled, though perhaps I was flattering myself. I told myself once more that he was my boss, but I wasn't sure how I could hold things back now, how I could keep my feelings out of it, stop plunging into it. In asking me about the sex, he was euphemistically asking me about the relationship and it struck me he was anxious for more. Or perhaps I'd got it completely wrong and he was just worried I'd pull a #MeToo and accuse him of exploiting me for sex in exchange for the job.

I walked out into the night air. My neighbour Carol was standing at her gate, looking up at a bright star next to a crescent moon.

'Hey, Christine, do you think that's Jupiter?'

'No, it's Venus,' I replied instinctively without even knowing. 'The planet of love.'

'Huh, there's no love in my house,' she said with a cackle.

'We'll just have to go to Mars then.' I was still giddy with the thought of Will.

The next day, I was so distracted I couldn't write my article. Cop on to yourself, I told myself briskly, it wasn't *Little Women* and I wasn't going to marry him. But when I checked Facebook, I spotted Will's latest post, and it was at that moment I understood everything. He was wishing all the *Belfast Telegraph* readers a merry Christmas and had posted a photo of his hearth with a roaring fire. On the mantelpiece, there was an arrangement of holly, fir boughs and silver pine cones – and right in the middle was my card. It was the only card there and it told me all I needed to know.

It told me that he cared.

Going Zero

Luke wakes up to a pungent earthiness that's stronger than ever. It takes him a moment to discover he's rolled from his sleeping bag face-first into the dirt. Like a pig sniffing out truffles, he jokes to himself. The birds seem to be singing paeans to the dawn. Turning his head, he can make out the rim of the trench and the trelliswork of trees patterning above it in the twilight. He lies a little longer, the branches reminding him of the calmes in a stained-glass window.

He sits up and reaches for his flak jacket and helmet. He normally keeps his battle rattle on while he kips but he made an exception last night as the flak jacket is too heavy when he lies, squeezing the life out of his lungs, and his mohawk feels like a mass of matted dreadlocks in that constant sweat-bowl of a helmet. All along the trench, the guys are starting to stir. A rat is sitting on a slumberer's hip, washing its paws, but Luke stares it down till it runs away.

'Men!' he shouts out. 'Let's do a clean-out. I want it de-ratted, not a crumb in sight.'

The notion flies through his head that it wasn't the food the rats smelt, but Big Mac's blood. However, he knows not to breathe of a word of it to his men. He climbs out of the trench, feeling that familiar second of vulnerability, all the more enhanced by the sight of yesterday's rugged craters thirty metres away. He crunches over shell fragments before hurdling over the felled, splintered trees, the sticky sap oozing out, coagulating. Luckily, there's still enough treeline to camouflage their trench. It's never good for troop morale when they have to fall back.

He takes a piss in the latrines, flies buzzing around him. He can hear the coo of that wood pigeon who only ever deigns to sit in the highest branches, like it's keeping watch over his men. The more he's up to his oxters in this forest, the more he's tuning into nature. Ten tons of Russian Smerches dumped on your head tends to keep you on the ball, he thinks ruefully to himself. These days, he's just a walking collection of sensations and isn't even sure if he can think logically anymore. It's scary how easy it is to lose yourself in the grey zone. Frontline madness, they call it, but he's counting every last day until he's on leave and prays nothing happens this time to make the Ukes delay it.

Outside the store tent, the lads are boiling water on gas rings. He checks on provisions, noting the lack of ready meals and coffee, so he radios through to the base.

'The one thing I can do for my lads is make sure they're well supplied,' he tells the base commander. 'The rockets I can do fuck all about, but hey.'

Big Mac's replacement arrives at eleven. A tall Dutch guy with a russet beard steps out of the SUV and introduces himself by his call sign, Bear. Luke shakes hands with him and takes off his helmet as he does on meeting all new recruits. He clocks the flare of surprise in Bear's eyes on registering the mohawk. Luke always uses his mad-looking mohawk as a means of garnering respect in the young killers he commands. Every single guy in the International Legion is a troubled character. Why else would they travel thousands of miles to fight for a country they'd barely heard of before the war? All soldiers say the same: 'I came because I couldn't stand the sight of defenceless Ukrainian women and children being bombed,' but Luke knows that those words of justification hide the real reasons: bloodlust, mercenary desire, escape from a failed marriage, a longing for death and glory, a need for expiation or a search for meaning.

It doesn't take long for Luke to run through the inventory of dos and don'ts.

'Whatever you do, Bear, no fires, no torchlight, no loud music, no shooting, no running away, no nothing,' Luke informs him. 'So here's the craic – all you do is wait. This war is a waiting game, nothing more. Patience wins the war because sooner or later the Russians always make a mistake. You might as well leave now if you think this is some computer game or a turkey shoot.'

Bear doesn't look happy. He keeps pinching his jawline uncertainly.

'In our recon unit, you don't even get to use your rifle,' continues Luke. 'Your job is to kill with your eyes, d'you understand? Your job is to soak up the pain of being shelled, to make the enemy expend all their ammo.'

'I know all about waiting,' Bear says. 'I was a sniper in Syria.'

'Well, think of yourself now as a sniper who doesn't pull the trigger.'

'Yes, sir.'

'Don't call me sir, call me Cool Hand. Now, show me your kit.'

He can smell the smoke from Bear's sleeping bag. He doesn't mind the soldiers smoking a bit of weed to help them sleep as long as they're not on watch. The smell puts him in mind of the music festivals where he worked for years on security. Sometimes, he thinks back to Glastonbury and the Electric Picnic: the tents, the outdoor ablutions, the unwashed clothes. The one difference now is he's at a festival where the only music is a deafening drum and bass. The firework display is a bit more explosive too.

'That's your bedroom,' he tells Bear, pointing into the trench.

It makes him sick to think it was only yesterday they hauled Big Mac out of that very spot, bleeding from his neck with the shrapnel. Big Mac was delirious by the time the field ambulance arrived. Reece MacDonald is his real name. The worst of it is he'd only just returned to the hot zone after marrying his fiancée.

'Lads, here's a bit of advice for you,' says Luke, raising his voice to address everyone. 'From now on, put your lives on hold – no marriages and no kids. Life plans are just tempting the gods of war to strike you down. I don't want to lose any more of you. In six months I've seen enough boots under blankets to last me a lifetime –'

A shout cuts across him from the soldier manning the radio.

'Incoming bird!' he yells.

Luke leaps down into the trench with the rest of his team. He glances across at Bear, glad to see him crouching down with the others. Back up to eight men now. One of the guys, Rambo, cracks his knuckles, almost pulling each joint out of its socket. The trilling of the birds gives way to a guttural, electrical whirr. They watch the drone's shadow wing its way over the broken-limbed trees. It slows down, monitoring yesterday's destruction. The shadow edges closer until the whirring is overhead. Luke's breath is so pent-up it feels as if nothing's entering his lungs.

The drone keeps hovering, its cameras zooming in. Has it spotted the tarpaulin? His spine stiffens in readiness for missiles, but the spy in the sky wanders back over the destroyed woodland, then swoops into the distance.

'Fuck off, you Ruscist cunts!' shouts Rambo. '*Slava Ukraini!*'

Luke keeps the men hunkered down until he deems it safe enough to prepare lunch.

'It's your lucky day, Bear,' he grins. 'A drone and no artillery.'

After lunch, Luke sits dozing in the heat. The sun is spearing between the firs and a sheared branch falls through a pine, the legacy of yesterday's shelling. The seed scales on the pine cones keep reminding him of pineapple hand grenades. Sometimes, when he listens to the birds, he wonders if they listen to the music of human voices with the same sense of pleasure. The fierce sunshine brings him back to that day last month when the Russian artillery line was blitzed into oblivion, leading to a glorious evening of respite with a barbecue, party tunes and, joy of joys, a skinny dip in the cool of the Donetsk River.

Out of the corner of his eye, he can see Rambo getting antsy with Bear about burying the rubbish. The guys are getting more and more short-tempered. Sooner or later, everyone gets trench-trap and losing fellow soldiers has wrenched the heart out of them. Luke can't wait to let off steam himself. Fighting or sex, it all works out the same way, through the body. As soon as he gets to Kyiv he's going to live it up, light the gelignite at both ends. The other guys say it's easy to meet a woman on Tinder and there is nothing he longs for more than to feel the lightness of his own naked body against another.

The man on radio duty jumps up. 'Russians spotted!'

Luke leaps out of his chair. 'Tell them to send the coordinates to the gun team. I'm on my way.'

He hurries through the trees and severed stumps, taking care to check for branches that might make a cracking sound underfoot. The danger of this dry August is that snapped wood can echo across the river like a gunshot. He sees the two forward observers lying embedded under some bushes and saplings at the river's edge. He gets onto his belly and crawls over to them, feeling the brambles pluck at his palms. From their spot, he looks out onto the river which is like one giant smooth tympanum, funneling echoes from miles away. He can already hear some faint shouts.

'Over there to the left,' one of the observers whispers to him.

He takes the binoculars and scans the river. The golden heat haze across the water makes it hard to locate anything. There are dark outlines of what appears to be driftwood, but he finally focuses in on the wet heads of six or seven swimmers.

'Bingo,' he says, taking in the undernourished shoulders and military buzzcuts.

He detects sudden movement and raises his binoculars up to the riverbank where an elderly fat woman is gingerly stepping down into the water, accompanied by two children.

'Fuck it,' he mutters. He double-checks the coordinates on the tablet and picks up the radio. 'Gun team, Cool Hand here. It's Russian soldiers alright. We request a fire mission.'

'Can you verify there are no civilians in the target range?'

Luke recognises the voice of that Ukrainian commander, Die Hard. Luke didn't like the man from the moment he met him. Die Hard kept pontificating to him about

Ukrainian rules of engagement while slapping his splay-fingered hand down on the table to emphasise his point. It's funny how a simple gesture can make you dislike someone. The real problem, though, is that Die Hard holds a grudge against Luke from the night they smoked out the Russians from the east of the river. Luke had been half-tore with the drink and had made a stupid error in inviting the gun team to a wrestling match and an even worse one in choosing to wrestle a military superior like Die Hard. He should never have lamped Die Hard in the eye, but he got carried away and the pride of his team was at stake. A week later, he was charged and fined a month's salary.

'Just wait while we verify,' Luke says. He prays that the babushka's about to leave the water, but she's swimming along, blissfully unaware of the danger, looking for all the world like a figure in a Monet painting. 'There's an elderly woman and two children,' Luke transmits regretfully. 'But they're not close to the target. At least fifty metres away.'

'No fire mission,' says Die Hard.

A spasm of rage overcomes Luke as he realizes that those skinny young Russians splashing each other like innocent kids were probably the men who injured Big Mac.

'Oh, come on,' Luke argues. 'They're not that close and, anyway, the Russians don't have any qualms about killing civilians.'

'Ukraine is better than that.'

'Yeah, and your moral superiority keeps getting us killed. One of my best guys was hit yesterday.'

'I'm sorry, Cool Hand.'

There is at least a recognition in Die Hard's voice that makes Luke hold back from letting blast, but he still resents how the gun team has it easier. All they do is sit deep in the forest, then drive into a field to fire before speeding away. They don't put their bodies on the line daily like the reconnaissance team.

Luke stares out one last time through the binoculars. He's envious of the Russians' squeals of fun in the fresh clear water. He imagines the buoyancy, the ineffable lightness, the feel of the light diamonding through the water to warm his limbs, the image of his own body ghostly and magnified like a long bluish iceberg under the surface. The flak jacket is heavier than ever on his back and he can smell this heady aniseed reek from the soldiers next to him. The air is stifling under the sun-baked bushes. His brains feel like boiled meat in a tin can.

His fingers tighten on the barrels of the binoculars, as he adjusts them to zone in on the face of a Russian. The Ukes call it 'going zero' when they're eye-to-eye with the enemy, but the Russian's gaze reflects nothing but sensory pleasure. It's strange to think that one tap on Luke's tablet could have killed this boy.

He crawls back to the tree cover. The one boon is that the likelihood of being shelled has melted away for a time. The pine needles and desiccated leaves are rusty red and pillow-soft under his boots. Out here, the low chant of the crickets is full of benedictions. Just a kilometre away, there are empty dachas and forest lodges from the summers when tourists flocked here. Just a tourist passing through, he tells himself. He won't let himself think about the winter ahead.

He pulls a thorn out of his wrist. He has so many scars now it looks like self-harm. It's odd that he came to Ukraine to be an army medic only to be assigned a spotter by the Ukrainians. They must have spied that restlessness in him. Through the trees, he can hear low singing and smiles to himself. Rambo is leading the men in harmonies of 'Keep Your Rifle by Your Side'. They sing it every time a soldier leaves their brigade. Yesterday they were too tired from clearing the shrapnel, too broken themselves to sing for Big Mac. Splintered branches had entered their trenches like darts and arrows, as if a native tribe had been attacking them,

'Beautiful, lads,' Luke calls out to them.

He can feel the emotion welling as images of Big Mac's cheerful grin swell in his mind. He's sure though that Big Mac has the spirit to make it out of hospital alive. He was always cracking jokes with his comrades like, 'I'm the sort to be on the beer, not on a bier.' There's nothing better than a bit of black humour to brighten the darkest days, to prompt laughter in the face of jeopardy.

Sometimes when his trench is immersed in the smokey miasma, a memory enters his head of the time as a teenager he'd stood in his parents' garden in Craigantlet watching a partial eclipse. That afternoon, the light had disappeared into half a minute of dusk, all birdsong quelled. It's odd how every bombardment brings the same sense of apocalyptic grandeur.

The sun's head is sinking fast now, a golden-haired child tired from being up so early. Luke lets a couple of lads go to forage for wild strawberries in a nearby clearing. Fresh fruit is rare on the frontline and they all savour these tiny succulent red hearts. Evening arrives early under the canopy and the gas stoves are fired up for dinner. He notices that Bear is cleaning his rifle in spite of knowing he'll never use it, but everyone has to find his own means of keeping busy. On the frontline you need the patience of a fisherman. The next shift of observers heads out to the riverside.

Just then, he hears it coming, a whistle through the air, accompanied by a split second of frantic bird wings.

'Get down!' he shouts but the words are swallowed by the explosion.

The guys hurtle down under the lip of the trench. Everywhere seems lit up by a sunrise. An automatic mortar is pounding the trees behind them, blast after blast, a rapid report. A 2B9, assesses Luke.

'Incoming ten metres behind us!' Rambo radios through to the gun team.

Luke searches for Bear and sees his face distorted in horror while the soldiers yell at full volume around him. He clambers over and shows him how to turtle, how to pull his helmet down over his head, compacting his body underneath. Blasts of fire start hitting the ground like meteorites. Getting closer. The margin between life and death can be a millimetre. Incendiary shells, clusters and clusters. 155 mill calibre, he estimates. Someone cries out in the trench as if hit, but Luke can't see who it is from the smoke. He realizes from the smell Bear's soiled himself.

'Scream!' he shouts, grabbing hold of Bear's arms and yelling into his face. 'Let it out! If you scream you don't shit or piss yourself!'

He screams himself and gets Bear to scream in the same rhythm, staring into his eyes, seeing the pupils dilate under frantic blinks, holding on to him, trying to keep the man's heart from combusting, trying to staunch the trauma in him because sometimes the gravest injuries are the ones that are unseen.

The explosions are punctuated with the retorts of a Javelin and the reply fortifies him until the moment the 2B9 starts up again and he feels as deserted to his fate as ever. Please let me stay alive, goes the refrain in his head. Bear keeps screaming into his face, coughing out the burnt air. With each successive boom, their bodies jolt into the air, swaying back and forth like they are dancing together. The ground keeps rising, soil is flung at them, spitting against their helmets. The acid smell of split pine fills the trench. Luke's heart is pounding to the rhythm of the blasts, his ears are throbbing, his eyes stinging, and an image of the Russians swimming in the halcyon sun-blessed river smokes into his shaken brain. He stares into Bear's blue eyes, but all he can see is the eyes of the Russian teenager, still full of beaming enjoyment as he presses the button to kill them all.

Homelands of the Tswana

Jack was driving home along the highway lined with flat acacia trees and blackened firebreaks. The Magaliesberg mountains lay blue in the mist to his left, but he didn't dare let his concentration lapse. A couple of township guys ambled across his path, forcing him to brake, but he was more bothered by a buckie towering with household possessions that kept swerving in front of him. Damn you, he exclaimed, guessing the guy was either dog-tired after a long day's drive or drunk.

At last, Jack turned off at Crocodile River reeking of human excrement into Mooinooi. At the traffic lights, a woman knocked at his window for change. It was impossible to tell her ethnicity from her sun-leathered face. He pulled away without giving her a coin and couldn't help noticing the disappointment in the sharp calcite of her eyes. So much need, too little money from his contract at the mine. The word 'contract' immediately bit home with treacherous spite.

He rattled onto the potholed clay road. There was a new billboard that said 'Top Choice Tombstones'. An oncoming car raised a translucent cloak of red dust that shimmered in the siren of the setting sun. Praise the Lord, he uttered out loud, for beating the blackout. He stopped at the entrance for Platinum Creek Gorge and pressed the button to open the gates. As he drove on, he sensed movement through the bushes and spotted a zebra. It cantered away when it saw him, showing a bloody gash on its hind leg. He hoped the leg was the work of jackals, but wondered even so, if it had been caught in a snare. Farms in the area had been reporting a rise in poachers.

His car crawled into the stony drive and Rosie and Max pelted round to the garage to bark their welcome. He could smell the sweetness of home in the lemongrass and lavender, making him think of Christly unguents.

'Hello, husband!' Maddie called from the kitchen.

'Hello, wife. Just let me ...'

He walked into the living room and radioed through to the farm owner, Zondra, about the injured zebra.

'Husband?'

He guessed from the way she was calling him husband she was about to wheedle him into helping her with dinner. Some husbands might hope to fling themselves into a chair after getting home, but she always wanted to put him to work. Still, he was pleased to see the freshly fried fat cakes on the counter. Liver and bacon tortoises, potatoes, onions and spinach were frying in the pan next to a pot full of squash. He couldn't help thinking, though, that hungry days were on the way.

'So, it's not good news –'

'Lisedi is just leaving,' said Maddie pointedly, cutting him off.

Lisedi emerged from the bathroom in her hi-vis jacket. It was important not to talk in front of the cleaning lady.

'Goodbye, Lisedi,' said Maddie. 'Have a good weekend.'

'Goodbye, Madam. You too.'

She was wearing a new maroon-red weave and, as she left, Jack could hear its silver beads tap together. A walking Newton's cradle, he said to himself, grinning.

'Will you squeeze some oranges?' asked Maddie.

'No problem at all.'

He managed to swallow down his annoyance, even though he'd been on his feet in the core yard half the day. He could feel the bulge of his blood vessels in one ankle and consciously pushed his weight onto the other. Varicose veins and he was only fifty-six.

'All ready to dish up,' announced Maddie before hollering, '*Sussetje*!'

Grace mooched languidly out of her room. With her online lessons and all those Chinese dramas she watched these days, she was never off her laptop. It seemed strange to him that a sixteen-year-old girl living on a game farm was so mentally secluded. She didn't share his robust physicality and he wondered if somehow the home schooling had enfeebled her or at least diminished her in a way that a normal knockabout school would have avoided. She used to swim in the dam with the other farm kids, but last summer Maddie scotched it as there were sightings of a leopard.

'Let's pray.' Jack held out his hands for Maddie and Grace to clasp. 'Blessed be this food to our bodies and our bodies to your service. Amen.'

The radio crackled in the background as they ate. Voices rendered indistinct with static mentioned something about a dead rhebok.

'Zondra said there was a fire earlier,' said Maddie, 'but the farm workers managed to put it out.'

He was always glad of the radio giving Maddie a window into the farm. Maddie used to run her own upholstery business but closed it down to help Grace with her interminable studies.

No sooner were the dishes packed away than the lights flipped off. Jack could hear the farm generators burst into animation. The easiest thing to do in the dim torchlight was play board games together. Grace chose Monopoly.

'Get ready to give me all your money, losers,' she boasted.

'Oh, listen to our young entrepreneur,' laughed Maddie.

He was almost grateful to the power cuts for allowing him to spend more time with Grace. He kept watching her, entranced by her pale skin constellated by honey-gold freckles, her blue eyes and copper-bright hair. In a way, it was glorious to have this living reminder of the pale, supple-limbed girl he'd married at twenty-seven. His own waist had expanded over the years but wasn't quite on a par with Maddie's, and when she was in good form, she'd joke about how her stomach resembled one of the sofa cushions she used to stuff.

'I'll take all your houses and hotels,' warned Grace. 'I'll even take over this house, I'll ...' Her words tailed off into a murmur. 'Beyoncé ... pink wash ...'

'*Sussie*, come back,' urged Maddie.

As the seconds passed, he watched Grace come back to life. It was always the strangest sensation to observe her brain reawakening. She'd had these petit mals since she was a toddler, her own personal blackouts, as it were. The neurologist had predicted she'd grow out of this form of absence epilepsy, but if anything it had become exacerbated by tiredness from being online all the time.

'"Beyoncé pink wash". What on earth's on your mind, *sussie*?' teased Maddie.

Grace looked bemused and embarrassed. 'Did I say that?'

As soon as the lights switched back on, the security alarm sounded. Maddie leapt to her feet to phone the armed response unit and confirm that everything was fine. Jack ended the game fast by making a series of reckless investments to ensure his bankruptcy. He grinned at Grace's dance of triumph.

'Right, it's nine o'clock,' he told her. 'One last C-drama, then to bed.'

He opened the door onto the stoop to let the dogs out. It had turned cold and beneath a sliver of a moon, Venus was shining like a diamond drill head.

In the bedroom mirror, he noticed heavy lines across his brow that made his face look as fractured as the core samples he logged at work. He tried to relax his features. At this rate, he'd be old before his time. He loosened his hair from its tie, changed into his pyjamas, strapped his knife belt round his waist and set his pepper spray on the bedside table. The rituals of bedtime. He often worried about not having a gun. Maddie had made him sell his rifle three years ago on the grounds of her religious pacifism. 'Surely you don't want to kill anyone,' she'd beseeched him, but there was a new spate of violent burglaries in North West Province that made such idealism seem naive. Even Pastor Ramesh was armed these days.

'What was 'the not good news' you had to tell me?' Maddie asked, now they were alone.

He teetered on coming clean but he was tired and scared of breaking down emotionally. 'Oh, I just meant I have to check the rigs on Saturday.'

'No problem. You can help me with the tomatoes and apricots when you come home.'

Good, she'd bought it. Now wasn't the time to discuss things when he hadn't even processed the news himself. That very afternoon, his boss had expended a lot of waffle on global forecasts and Jack's 'sterling work in the field of mine exploration', but the fact remained that Jack's contract wasn't going to be renewed. Jack had been a boss himself until two years ago. The irony was he'd left his job in management to try and cure the gnawing stress, only to end up on temporary contracts racked with insecurity.

He turned the light out. Maddie shifted on her pillow. In the moon-shot dark he could hear the cracking of the corrugated roof as it cooled and the brisk pads of the dogs pounding on the dry earth. He reminded himself to water the garden this Saturday now that the spring sun was crisping the grass. Outside, Rosie was barking head off with Max in bass accompaniment. Perhaps that skin-and-bone bok had returned to browse on their bushes.

The dogs settled and he turned over onto his side. It only ever took him seconds to fall asleep.

The cockerel next door was crowing. Twilight was entering the cracked window, the edges stippled with condensation. Bafani tried to get up off his mattress, but fell back, drunk with sleep. He hugged his blanket close into him, trying to blot out the sound of bubbling water. When he raised his head and opened his eyes, his cousin Obonye was hunched over the gas ring, the low flame licking its blue tongue round the pot.

'Hurry up. I've got to go work,' said Obonye, passing him a cup.

After drinking down the watery mealies, Bafani ran out for a shit and piss into his bucket at the edge of the open sewer. He squatted behind a rock, but two hens wandered over to him, clucking, and he gave them a tap with his boot to go away.

'Why are you watching me?' he muttered.

'Come on!' yelled Obonye.

Bafani wiped himself with a piece of the Mooinooi paper, then emptied his bucket into the sewer and quickly rinsed it out. He followed Obonye to the roadside. The satellite dishes on the roofs of the tin pondoks shone like a million moons in the rising sun. Sellers were lifting sacks of onions onto their stalls; one vendor was busily turning chicken on a braai. Bafani's eyes searched through the dusty grass for yesterday's fruit. He picked up a discarded avocado.

'Don't,' grumbled Obonye. 'You make it look like I never feed you.'

The avocado was so soft he ripped it open with his fingers. The interior was greying, blackening in parts, well past its best, but he managed to scavenge a few delicious bites.

Obonye had edged over to a makeshift fire. It was odd, thought Bafani, how someone damaged by fire was still drawn to its heat. One side of Obonye's face resembled ridged bark, the melt marks runnelled into his skin, and the fingers on his right hand were little more than stumps. The cause of it had been a rogue petrol bomb during the Mandela Day riots some years ago, but there was a blessing even in the worst of injuries because if Obonye hadn't suffered from fire himself he might never have let Bafani move into his shack.

The taxi van shuddered into view and Obonye made the sign for Sibanye mine where he worked as a car guard. He and Bafani clambered into the seats behind the driver. The mine workers were in the back, yawning, conserving energy for the day ahead. The taxi shuttled past a smelter, the ironwork latticing its way into the sky, steam and smoke belching out of the concrete tower. The smell of sulphur was overpowering, but in a minute they'd get used to it. Next, they passed the opencast chrome mine.

'Stop here!' Bafani called out to the taxi driver and fist-bumped Obonye goodbye.

He left the road and walked onto some disused land mounded with dark rubble. He was the first to arrive, so he took a minute to let his eye rove round for a good spot and was rewarded with three shiny black chrome-seamed stones that clinked satisfyingly into his bucket. The sweet music of money, he sang to himself. His hands were freezing and the sun's rays felt like a heartless tease, a false promise of warmth.

He hunkered down, switching to autopilot as he sifted through the stony harvest. His mind flickered back to the fire at his aunt's house four months ago. He'd lived with her for years but had been out drinking the night the fire started. Although he hadn't witnessed it, he couldn't stop imagining her cries, her confusion. He tried to beat it out of his mind, stamp on it as you would snuff out a burning ember, but oh, if only he'd been there to help her put it out. He'd told her to be careful of candles during the blackout. He'd arrived back from the shebeen to see the smouldering remains of her house while ashes whirled around in the wind like a morbid tickertape.

Fortunately, his aunt wasn't hurt, but she had left for Cape Town to live with a distant relative. Sometimes he berated himself for thinking about the loss of his documents in that fire more than his aunt, though the consequences had been huge as he could no longer work in the mine. When he'd gone to the Home Office to see about renewing his ID, he'd insisted he was South African born and bred, pure Tswana. How could he not have been Tswana, being so fine-featured? The official, sitting there like a big bloated wildebeest, had told him it would cost two thousand rand. Corrupt fucking bastard.

'How can I get two thousand rand for an ID card if I haven't got the necessary ID to earn it?'

'That's what they call catch-22, my friend,' shrugged the official. 'Next!'

Bafani hadn't wanted to do anything illegal, but that same day he'd gone back to Obonye's shack and talked through the options. Obonye had suggested buying fake clocking-in cards and hiding in the mine until closing time to steal the copper piping.

'Copper fetches a fine price these days,' Obonye pointed out.

But there was one serious hitch. At night, the mine's water was switched off meaning the quartzite dust could cut your lungs to shreds. The risk of getting caught paled into significance next to living with damaged lungs for the rest of your life.

The sound of stones in buckets brought him back to the present. Other scavengers had shuffled onto the dark shoreline and some were sedulously digging with spades. Bafani pulled his jumper off, feeling the heat of the sun on his back. He imagined he was on a vast sandy beach of whelk pickers. Even though he'd never been to the sea, he knew it well from TV.

'Look over there,' said a woman nearby.

He turned to see a camera crew at the foot of one of the slag heaps. Dancers were moving in formation through the far-off haze. Music videos were always being filmed here as it was the closest thing you'd get to an apocalyptic landscape, and it gave him a yearning in his heart, wishing he was part of their glamorous world instead of toiling on this wasteland. He dropped back onto his haunches, searching for the glimmering black. Bit by bit, like an ant eats an elephant, he told himself.

A dassie scampering past paused to watch him, gnawing hungrily at its paws.

'I'm starving myself, man,' he told it.

When the sun was at its highest, he stood up, stretched his back and drank from his water bottle. He walked over to the flattened earth by the roadside and unwrapped the rusks Obonye had given him that morning. He licked every single crumb off the newspaper, then sat a while listening to the birdsong by the raggedy bushes next to the smelter.

At three o'clock, the silver 4x4 came and opened up its boot. Bafani carried over one bucketful, then another.

'Nice work,' said the driver, counting out seventy rand.

'I thought it would be more.'

'The price of chrome is going down every day.'

'Want to earn real money?' shouted the guy from the passenger seat, whose golden baseball cap was jauntily askew.

'Yeah.' Bafani went round to the open window.

The golden-capped guy was chewing on a short plastic straw. 'How fast you need it?'

'Now. No, yesterday.'

The guy passed him a card. 'Phone me.'

'What sort of work do you have?'

'Don't ask questions, man. You need money, call me.'

The 4x4 drove off, raising a dust that made Bafani cough in its wake. He tied his jumper tight around his waist and traipsed towards the main road, his empty bucket rhythmically slapping against his calf. He passed the lake in the old chrome quarry pit and stopped off to stare down into its cloudy jade depths. There was a rumour that it was so deep it was a perfect place for dumping bodies.

Jack was trapped behind a convoy of crushers leaving the mine. It was four pm and he was impatient to get home after hours in the metal maze of the core yard. He glanced left at one of his drill rigs – and hell! He recognized that silver 4x4 turning out of the track. He immediately reversed and headed down to the rig himself. The silence struck him as he parked. The men were packing up.

'What's going on?' he asked, perturbed.

'A guy in a gold baseball cap told us to give him a thousand rand or go home,' explained the foreman. 'He said he was from the local community.'

'You can't stop drilling. We have to be finished here by Sunday.'

He phoned the office to warn them the henchmen were back claiming that the mine belonged to the Tswana tribe and asking for rent. It was the second time in a fortnight. There were rumours that a Marikana politician was encouraging squatters to expand onto the land. All these gangsters trying to fleece money off the mine like oxpeckers on a giraffe's back.

As he drove away, he told himself it wasn't his problem. His contract wasn't going to be renewed next month. He was out on his ass and disastrous as it was, at least he wouldn't have to deal with these blackmailers.

He drove into Marikana over the speed ramps and past church tents and car washes. The road was flooded from a burst pipe, his wheels churning up mud. Young teenagers were sitting at the outdoor tables of Asta La Vista shebeen. They couldn't have been much older than fourteen and he tutted out loud, comparing them to Grace sitting in her bedroom immersed in her laptop. Women were walking along the street in their slippies under brightly coloured parasols; one woman was sitting nonchalantly on the horizontal branch of a stunted tree as if it was a garden seat fashioned especially for that purpose. A man ahead was driving his skinny cattle forward with a *sjambok*, forcing cars to slow down.

It didn't take long though to reach the orange groves. The smog began to clear and the forecast was for warmer wind in the next few days as the snow melted in the Drakensberg. The fields were lined with pivots, stretching out like the diaphanous wings of giant dragonflies. He began to smile on the way into Mooinooi at how the wild pear trees were blooming on the koppies.

He sped up after checking the time on the dashboard. Maddie got irritated at his lateness and always impressed on him that his real job was his family. She seemed jealous of his work time, tied as she was to Grace's schooling, but he realized with a pang she'd soon have him all to herself. When he turned into the driveway, Maddie and Grace were already waiting outside the garage with huge pots of mince and rice.

'We'll have to hurry,' said Maddie reproachfully as they packed the boot.

On their journey to Brits, he flicked on the radio for Grace. He never listened to music himself, but Maddie liked rap and rock, as long as it wasn't too outlandish.

'I want to go see this band in Joburg,' said Grace.

'Humph.' He caught himself uttering this all the time now Grace was getting older and craving adult things, but he immediately rowed back on it as the last thing he wanted was for her to grow into a solitary oddity. 'Well, maybe we can take you and a friend.'

'Open your heart,' derided Maddie of one set of romantic lyrics. 'The only person I'd let my heart be opened by is a registered surgeon.'

The road sign said 'Hijacking Hotspot!' and Jack accelerated. He'd heard at the mine that only slow cars got rammed off the road. The mellow afternoon sun was turning the Magaliesberg a soft pink. By the time they reached the municipal dump, the buildings were casting dark rectangles on the asphalt.

'Stinks,' said Grace.

Pastor Ramesh and the other church elders were already setting up tables in the car park. Zondra, ever the organizer, assigned Jack his table. Whenever Zondra fed people at the dump, she always dressed in African finery with a shell necklace, wooden hoop earrings and a colourful shawl, conveniently dismissing her Boer ancestry.

The dump-dwellers stopped scouring the ground and began making their way down to the car park. Others exited their cardboard and plastic shelters and shoved past each other to be first in line. It struck Jack that these men had the same smell as wild game.

'Please stand in an orderly queue,' Pastor Ramesh called out in the amplified tone he employed in his sermons. 'There's enough for everyone.'

Jack gulped down a helping of mince while Maddie and Grace started serving. The polystyrene boxes were almost snatched out of their hands. Forks were discarded as filthy fingers shoveled the food into mouths. It was clear these men hadn't had a meal in days.

'Hey, sexy lady,' said one man in a low voice, looking over Grace as hungrily as others looked over the food. 'Want to bouncey-bounce?'

Jack stepped forward, outraged. 'Oy.'

'*Sussie*, go and stand at the back,' Maddie told Grace.

Jack was still staring at the man. Intimidated, the guy took his beanie off before holding his hands out to receive his rice. Something jingled on the ground. A crack pipe had fallen out of his beanie. Heavenly God, thought Jack.

In less than an hour, they were packing up to leave.

'Doesn't it feel good to be so close to these poor men?' trilled Zondra in some sort of charity-inspired ecstasy. 'Makes us appreciate how much we all have.'

Jack felt a stab of pain from envisaging the pity she'd soon be lavishing on him and hurried away under the pretext of getting back before dark.

On the drive home, there was a fire in the bushveld. The coral trees that lined the highway were as bright orange in the sunset as the streaks of fire that rampaged alongside them. Smoke ballooned across the tarmac and the air tasted acrid. As the sun turned into a hazy red circle like the tip of a cigarette, all Jack could think of was the crack pipe falling out of the man's hat.

A song was playing on the radio but he didn't register it until Maddie took umbrage.

'Eesh! I'm not having that weird drugs song playing any more,' she said, turning it off.

'What drugs?' protested Grace. 'The song's about achieving your potential.'

'Well, he sounds like he's on drugs, so I'm not having it.'

'Oh, come on! It's cool!'

'Hey, hey, stop arguing,' he snapped. 'Or I'll give you something to really worry about.'

'What do you mean?' asked Maddie, perplexed. 'Husband?'

He hadn't meant to talk about it until they were home, but all that inconsequential squabbling was too much to take.

'Let's leave it till later,' he said, keeping his eyes on the dusking highway.

The following afternoon, Bafani took the long walk through Marikana. In Zone 6, he noticed some new builds with elaborately pillared stoops. These were palaces compared to the pondoks, but they were prisons too with bars on the windows. Wild pink magnolia was growing gloriously on the walls, but it didn't hide the fact these were township houses. A lizard leapt onto a dog lazing on one of the stoops. The dog's wide-eyed spasm of shock made Bafani burst into laughter.

As the sun sank behind the roofs, a brothel door opened and two beautiful women tripped out, hair thick as the nests of weaver birds.

'Hey, boy,' one of them called out with a smile, but the other took him in at one glance right down to his skinny locust legs and chrome-dusted sweater, and looked away disdainfully.

He felt it keenly and it steeled him to get to his meeting on time. The problem was that the security lights looming over Marikana couldn't cut through the smoke of the open-air fires. He panicked that he'd lost his way, but at the next turning, he saw a sign on a tree trunk:

Need Help?
Penis Enlargement
Lost Lovers
Pregnancy Problems
Lottery
Remove Bad Luck
Phone Dr O 744-412

He finally spotted the white cloth hanging from a roof. 'Dr Obadiah – Herbalist' was painted above the *muti* hut door. He swallowed hard, scared suddenly. All those rumours about itinerants being slaughtered so their blood and organs could be used for potions. He just hoped he was worth more to them alive than dead. He knocked on the door. Dr Obadiah, looking the perfect part of a *sangoma* in his white shirt and tribal hat, invited him into a lamplit room draped with animal skins and a thicket of antlers, then led him through to a plainer office.

Golden-Cap was lounging back on the office chair, his feet on the desk.

'Take a seat,' he said, noticing that Bafani's eyes were drawn to two buffalo horns nailed to the wall. 'You like them?'

'Yeah, amazing.'

Golden-Cap smiled, showing a gold-capped side tooth.

'Good. Game is our game. Let's talk, but if you tell a soul about us, we will curse you, your mother, your brothers, your sisters, your babies. Do you believe in the power we have?'

'Yes,' said Bafani, even though he felt the twist of scepticism on his tongue. He feared men more than magic.

'Good. Have you ever shot a gun or used a knife?'

'Of course.' Growing up in Marikana, he'd shot a rifle a few times as a kid. 'But I don't want to kill anyone.'

'Kill?' Golden-Cap laughed. 'We don't want you to murder anyone. You'll only be killing animals that are going to be culled anyway by a rich farmer. These game farms should be part of our homelands. You're a Tswana aren't you?'

'Yes.'

'So, it's only taking what's ours by nature and God's right. You'll be paid by the animal. If you help us get a zeb – two thousand rand outright. We'll pick you up tomorrow midnight at the fever tree. The one on the road to Mooinooi.'

'Fine. I know it.' Everyone knew that fever tree with its eerie shade of green bark.

'Ok, tomorrow,' said Golden-Cap with a dismissive waft of his hand.

As Bafani left, he caught sight of himself in a mirror framed by bok hide. He seemed blurred, not his full self. He stumbled down the steps onto a dark dirt track and almost knocked over a woman with a baby in a sling.

'Sorry, sorry,' he mumbled. 'Didn't see you.'

He passed the lights of the Love and Peace Tavern and longed for a beer and a plate of Russian and chips. Under an outdoor table, a skinny pavement mutt curled himself up from the cold like a boerewors. Bafani stopped off at the *spaza* shop and bought some chicory coffee as a treat for Obonye and, in a rush of spontaneity recollecting Dr Obadiah's sign, a lottery ticket. He remembered someone telling him how vulture blood was used in lottery spells because vultures were able to see from afar.

He thought excitedly of all the food he could buy for himself and Obonye, trying to quell the imagined words of his aunt who would have implored him not to have anything to do with this gang. 'But I need the ID card,' he retorted and the self-justification kept growing until he told his aunt to fuck herself. With an ID card, he would be a person again, legitimate, visible, and he'd get that job in the mine and rise up the ranks until he had a house with a big stoop and a portico, somewhere that would make his aunt proud of him. And yet, part of him knew she'd be ashamed of his greed.

Back at the shack, Obonye was grilling chicken. Bafani sat down beside him, feeling the hunger crack through his belly like a giant chasm.

'Where have you been?' Obonye asked.

'Oh, nowhere. Just thinking about things.'

He handed Obonye the coffee and lottery ticket. He told himself if God saw fit to let Obonye win the lottery tonight he'd renounce all connection with the gang.

'Let's *maak 'n plan*,' Jack said to Maddie as he strode out to the garden with some netting and bamboo sticks.

The garden was a mass of birdsong. The go-away bird was yelling its gravelly call and there was a sonorous note in the background as steady as a heart rate monitor. Two-seater planes kept flying overhead as they always did on a

Saturday afternoon. He could smell the flowers on the tangerine tree and the strawberries ripening in their beds. He threw the netting over the trees, the green ovals of new apricots gladdening his heart.

It had been a sleepless night for both himself and Maddie, beset with mortgage fears. Maddie was particularly worried about having to let Lisedi go as she relied on her salary with them. However, in the morning while he was out at the rigs, Maddie began taking control, phoning around family and friends to impart the news that her upholstery business was up and running again.

'We have to make this business work as a business,' Maddie had impressed on him, making him understand they needed to be more ruthless moneywise than in the past.

Rosie scampered over to him, tail drumming in her desire to be stroked.

'At least everything is ok in your world,' he mumbled. 'Born with your bum in the butter, weren't you?'

He sat down with her on the stoop and took in how the mountains were full of silvery pleats and folds. Nearby, Maddie was picking a bouquet of orange fire lilies and wild irises to bring into the house and he felt a wave of love for her. The sun had no strength in it, but there was just enough heat in the breeze to feel like spring. Tomorrow, he told himself, he'd irrigate the grass and scythe down a new firebreak round the house. The aloe vera was becoming a hazard.

He went indoors to take the ice cream and a tub of cape gooseberries out of the freezer. The radio was echoing with the warning that a fire had swept through a nearby game farm. Every dry windy August and September, a few Tswana would try to burn down the farms, encouraged by avaricious politicians who wanted their tribal lands back. He dismissed the thought, scooping out ice cream for

Maddie and Grace, wondering if he could eke it out for another turn. But so what if they indulged in a last bit of luxury? After all, Christ had elected to have his feet rubbed with expensive ointment, telling his disciples, 'The poor will be around forever, but you only have me for a short time.'

He realised he wouldn't be able to buy that rifle he wanted, but with Maddie so against guns it was probably for the best. Still, he had the paintball gun from the time he'd shot at that big bull nyala who kept eating their figs. On a whim, he walked out to the garage to find it.

'Come on, *sussie*,' he called out to Grace. 'Let's get you away from that laptop.'

Together they stepped over the garden fence into the bush. The crickets were chorusing, a hadeda cawing overhead. He handed Grace the paintball gun and told her to hit a boekenhout tree fifteen metres away.

'Shoot standing, then kneeling, then do it running forward,' he told her.

With her first few shots she missed, but soon the bark was splattered in red paint and he was pleased to see her sprinting and firing with gusto.

'Atta girl,' he said, taking the gun off her and reloading it. 'My turn.'

He used the sights to hit into the heart of the trunk and sank onto his left knee without breaking aim. He fired again and again, seeing his boss's face before him, releasing his shots with more and more angry venom. Next, he charged towards the tree, pumping paint into its red bark, blitzing it, massacring it, unleashing all his frustration and pain into a few moments of exhilaration, and he heard Grace shout out behind him in remonstration, but he kept attacking at close range, remorselessly splintering its core until the very last paintball was spent.

The silver 4x4 picked Bafani up at the fever tree. He'd almost broken his ankle getting there, stumbling over roots along the dark road, but it was at least preparation for heading out to the game farm. There were four of them in the car: Bafani, the driver, Golden-Cap and a poacher called Welfare.

'I used to do rhino patrol in Pilanesberg,' Welfare told him, 'until I found out how to make better money.'

The road was empty at ten pm except for some trucks. By chance, they found themselves behind a buckie from the Anti-Poaching Unit.

'Praise fucking be,' said Bafani when the buckie turned off into a farm.

Golden-Cap laughed and chewed vigorously on his straw. 'They can't do nothing to us. The police are in our pocket.'

They came to a large sign saying 'Platinum Creek Gorge'. The wind was kicking up dust and the headlights made it look like a white sandstorm.

'It's good that there's some wind tonight,' said Welfare, passing Bafani a belt with a long, thick knife to strap around his waist. 'A poacher's moon too.'

They crawled to a stop at the edge of an electric perimeter fence. There was enough natural light from the moon to outline the trees and bushes. Blossom glowed on the acacias and, curiously, the dry grass bore a luminous chalk-like quality.

Golden-Cap pulled a bag of wire snares from the boot, then handed a rifle to Welfare who slung it across his shoulder. The driver stayed in the car while the other three crept over to the ditch. After five minutes their contact, a tenant from one of the farm flats, arrived and let them into the back of his car. Once inside the game farm, they slipped out and disappeared into the veld. Bafani could feel the bushes tear at his face and put his forearm up as a shield. Sharp twigs snagged his sweater, as if it didn't have enough holes already.

'Here's a good place,' said Welfare, stopping. 'The nyala graze here at first light before going to drink at the dam.'

They waited for Welfare to lay snares at certain points in the undergrowth. The plan was to come back the next night to check if they'd caught anything.

'Look,' said Golden-Cap, alerting them to something white in the grass. 'A leopard was here. See? Its shit is white from eating bones.'

Bafani shivered. A nightjar was calling and there was a thrashing sound in the high grass. They moved away stealthily. Further on, Golden-Cap insisted on stopping for a smoke break.

'Prices are flying through the roof. Bok horns can fetch a hundred and fifty dollars online,' said Golden-Cap. 'Hides are sixty.'

'The price of meat's rocketing,' replied Welfare. 'I know a guy who says *muti* blood is going for a thousand rand.'

'Bullshit, man, we can get more than that.'

The low diesel purr of a farm vehicle could be heard in the distance and they fell quiet.

'What we really need is that zeb hide,' whispered Golden-Cap. 'Let's get it.'

Welfare and Golden-Cap moved cautiously through the silhouettes of bushes till they reached a house partly illuminated by a security light. Bafani, following them, found it odd that no dogs were barking. Beside the garden fence, a raasblaar was rustling loudly in the wind. Golden-Cap pointed out the zebra hide and the blesbok skull and horns which were hanging from the wooden wall on the stoop. Welfare had already hopped over the fence.

'You get the blesbok, Bafani,' whispered Golden-Cap, aiming his handgun at the stoop doors. 'I'll cover you.'

Bafani climbed into the garden. The house was mostly in darkness but the beat of his trainers on the earth were in crazy synch with his pulse. He spotted the carcass of a small white dog beside the stoop and the terrible realisation hit him that it had been poisoned.

He tried not to make a sound as he stepped onto the concrete. He slinked in under the blackness of the eaves and lifted his hands up to the horns, not daring to breathe. His heart was pounding like rhino hooves. Next to him, Welfare had expertly detached the zebra skin and was slipping away from the shadows.

A light flicked on in the house. Bafani gripped hard on the skull and used his knife to try and prise the mount from the wall, but it was caught on a nail and he tugged on it again and again in spite of its rattles, knowing he needed to take it because if he didn't, he'd never be hired again. The sliding doors opened and a man stepped out with a knife in his hand. In the half light, the man's hair was long and wild like an Old Testament prophet, his eyes ablaze with fear and anger. A woman was calling out from inside.

In that split second, Bafani thought of stabbing the man, of running, of screaming, but there was something in the man's hesitation that recognised the skull wasn't worth dying over, and instead Bafani made a final yank to free it from the wall. The house alarm began to ring. A gunshot rang out from Welfare's rifle, the bullet smashing through glass, but Bafani turned blindly and ran back to the fence, leaping over it, catching his foot and falling cumbersomely, feeling a massive pain in his side followed by a wetness.

'Shit, I'm bleeding!' he shouted out, realizing he'd been gouged by the horn. An image of Christ speared in his stomach seared through his mind.

'Run!' said Golden-Cap, picking up the skull and pulling him to his feet.

Bafani raced after him into the bush, the adrenaline driving away the pain as he smashed through the branches.

'Welfare, where's Welfare?' Golden-Cap asked, turning.

As Bafani looked back, he could see Welfare crouching, using his lighter to set fire to the tinder of the grass. The wind fanned and flared the fire and it surged into the parched bushes.

'No!' Bafani shouted.

'Leave him, he'll find us,' said Golden-Cap. 'Let's go.'

By the time Bafani got to the perimeter fence, he could smell the smoke. He looked back through the sparse bushveld to where the fire was licking round the upper columns of the stoop and stretching into its eaves. The land was so dry it was like it had been waiting to be ignited.

'Oh God,' he moaned, praying for the prophet-man.

Welfare jogged up to him, the zebra hide slung over his shoulder like he was a warrior chief. 'Don't even think about those people. This is Tswana land!' he brayed triumphantly.

Golden-Cap picked up two forked branches and used them to push aside the electric wires. As Bafani moved towards the wire, he could see a dark splotch of his own blood hitting the moonlit ground, putting his mark on it. The fire crackled behind him, oranging the sky, blowing embers into the black.

Sexploits of a Rooftopper

I've always loved being single. For a start, you've the freedom to shout unwoke slurs at the TV without being chided by your partner. And you don't have to hide what you Google. My friend Sally, for instance, conceals her penchant for porn from her husband by surfing the middle-class portals of classical art. She reckons the best countries for erotic art are India, Thailand and Burma. Recently she was telling me about this Indian painting of a god pleasuring two ethereal-looking women with his toes.

But since getting together with a Dutchman, Aart, I found myself changing, wanting to spend more and more time with him. We started seeing each other at weekends, but then it was Thursdays too, even the occasional Monday, and gradually it turned into a long weekend, then to a week and in no time it ended up a long week, and this probably sounds ridiculous to everyone who isn't a commitment-phobe, but for me it was radical.

It was his kindness in the smallest of things that won me over, like the way he carried my shopping bags. He wasn't just a human handbag – he was tall, hazel-eyed and had black hair, deliciously grey-flecked at the sides. He also had large shoulders with armpits you could nestle into for hours.

After four months together, he told me he had to go back to the Netherlands for three weeks as his mother wasn't well. I was glad to book his flights for him. I was working in Trailfinders as a travel consultant, while studying for my Ph.D. in Troubles literature, and could get fifty per cent discount. Strangely, I hadn't even booked any holidays for myself because I was happy being home with him most days.

One of the best things about Aart was I could be more honest with him than any of my previous men. The day before he left for Eindhoven, I admitted that one of my guilty pleasures was watching YouTubes of daredevil stunts going wrong and all he did was widen his eyes a micro-fraction and say, 'Show me.' So, we wound up watching lots of ludicrous mishaps together including a Japanese rooftopper who fell off a skyscraper.

'He'll need another type of scraper to lift him off the road,' joked Aart darkly.

It was great having someone with a humour as black as mine. I explained to him that my reason for watching these images was to feel alive.

'I can show you how to feel alive,' he murmured, nuzzling into my neck. 'I've been looking up something myself. Want to try something new?'

'Sure thing.'

'It's called 'the knuckle' and I read about it in a tantric manual,' he said, his hands moving round to undo my belt.

I loved how he kept reading things to bring pleasure into my life. I'd caught him with his nose in a Marquis de Sade in the first days of our relationship and had been a bit worried, but luckily he hadn't whipped, slapped or attempted to strangle me. So far at least.

After sex, Aart kept fooling around with my right nipple.

'Can I take this to Eindhoven with me?' he asked with a grin.

'You'd get bored of it. You'd probably end up using the hoover on it.'

'No, I wouldn't,' he said, giving my breast a last kiss. 'But I better go pack.'

At the front door I wanted to say I'd miss him, but it seemed needy and I wasn't keen on coming across as reliant on him, so I just said, 'So long.'

'Be careful,' he said, though I think he meant take care.

'I'll be grand.'

'I know. As we say in Dutch, 'weeds never die',' he teased. He promised to send me some stroopwafels in the post. I watched him get into his car and waved him off, stepping out into the street to see his departing tail lights, standing there till they'd disappeared from sight.

The next day, I went to work at Trailfinders. June was the beginning of our busy season and the phones were off the hook.

'I'm really into indigenous art,' a customer told me. 'What country can you recommend?'

'I've heard India, Thailand and Burma are excellent for local art,' I replied.

I spent an hour with her, going over her demands before she finally booked for Peru. I know it sounds childish but I gave her trip the code ARSI1 in recompense for being so difficult. All of us consultants made up insulting codes for customers who made you tear your hair out. When my boss saw it at the end of the day, she rolled her eyes somewhat but let it pass. After a year of dealing with our flippancies, she'd developed the rictus smile of a Halloween pumpkin. I felt almost sorry for her.

I was heading for the bus after work through the graffiti-ridden underpass when I clocked him. Ryan in his biker jacket, fretted punk t-shirt, black jeans and zipped boots, sporting a gelled quiff. Belfast was so small you couldn't avoid anyone, not that I wanted to avoid him. I seemed to bump into him once a year and invariably invited him back to mine for sex – it was like having an annual MOT. And it always seemed to be at the height of June fecundity. My Midsummer Man, it suddenly occurred to me.

'How you doing, Megan?' he greeted me, his mischievous blue eyes lighting up.

'Great.' I pointed to his sexy leather wristbands. 'You look like Maximus in *Gladiator*,' and even as I said it, I was thinking Gluteus Maximus and what a terrific arse he had.

Of course, he wasn't perfect. He was selfish in bed and I didn't mean sexually. One time, he took up the whole bed, consigning me to its polar outreaches. I nearly fell out during the night. But no one was perfect.

I walked with him out of the underpass into the evening sunshine. A gust of wind blew the petals from the trees, sending them flying across the street like a flotilla of white butterflies set loose from their tethers.

'Look,' he said, showing me his phone. 'It's my newborn Caitlin. Isn't she beautiful?'

I was taken aback. 'I didn't know you were with anyone, Ryan.'

'I'm not. Fancy going out tonight?'

'Ah, well ...' I glanced across at the tables outside McHugh's Bar and it was tempting, all these drinkers sitting with silvery mojitos so filled with mint leaves they looked like jars of salad.

'Oh, go on,' he urged. 'We don't have to go too wild. Sure, I need a pack of antacids after two pints these days!'

And I was thinking how hot he was and how I wouldn't be able to resist after two beers, so I answered, 'I can't cause you know how you said you weren't with anyone? Well, I am.'

He looked surprised as he never thought I'd abandon the fraternity of the free.

'Ah, that's a pity,' he said. 'But I'm sure I'll see you again.'

I wasn't so sure myself.

In the days after meeting Ryan, I couldn't stop thinking of him as a dad. I found myself entertaining wild notions of having Aart's child and wistfully glanced at pregnancy test kits when I was in Boots, even though Aart and I used condoms. We'd even tried femidoms but they were huge and it felt like having a paddling pool inserted into my vagina. Aart was in his late thirties and separated with two kids, so I wasn't sure how he'd feel about more children, but the fusion of his dark hair with my golden red would make a stunning auburn I felt.

The thing was, he'd shaken my faith in living alone. I was thirty-two and it struck me how hideous it would be to die on my own in my rented house to some ludicrously tragic obituary. I'd read those ones in the *Guardian*: 'She leaves behind a husband and two children'. In my case it would be 'She leaves behind fuck all' or, even worse, 'She leaves behind a house spider and a potted plant'.

Aart had already broached living together and I could see now how stupid I'd been to turn him down. He was Mr Stability too. He worked as a pharma-lab supervisor and, let's face it, working in state-sponsored drugs he'd never be unemployed. It was almost as secure as working in the arms industry.

Aart WhatsApped me a few times the first week he was away, but then didn't get back for a couple of days. Even when he did, there was no sign of the stroopwafels. At first, I put it down to the slow Dutch postal service, though I figured that being so close to Germany it was probably highly efficient.

When you're back from the Netherlands, I can't wait to visit your own nether regions I WhatsApped him, trying to make him smile.

A few hours later he replied with a rolling on the floor laughing emoji and I was glad.

When Aart returned to my house, he looked different. His hair was longer on top and close-shaved at the sides and the way it pinpricked my fingers when I touched it felt divine. His face had a healthy tan.

'So, did you have a good time without me?' he asked.

'Course I did. I watched loads of YouTubes – there was a great one of an acrobat falling off a tightrope.'

'Ah, if only I'd been here,' he teased.

'And how's your mother?'

'Ok, good,' he said vaguely. 'Better than I thought.'

'What happened to the stroopwafels?'

'Sorry, ran out of time.'

He sat down in the armchair, distracted. It seemed strange as he habitually sat next to me on the sofa, barely able to keep his hands off me. Now I thought about it, he always went straight to the kettle to make coffee when he arrived. And then I got it. He was sitting awkwardly, perched forward, and 'the big talk' was coming. I could sense him summoning up the will to be authoritative. It reminded me of the time my school principal invited me into his office to tell me I was suspended. Or the time my landlady asked me to leave her house for partying too much. Christ, I've been told off a lot in my life!

'So, I have to tell you,' he began. His hands were clasped and I knew what was coming, not that I was used to it as I'd always endeavoured to be the dumper, not the dumpee. 'I met up with a friend I hadn't seen in a few years. The last time I saw her we were at a jazz festival and shared a drunken embarrassing night.' His hand rose inadvertently to his lips to stop himself breaking into a grin. 'Anyway, just as I arrived in Eindhoven, she Facebooked me out of the blue.'

That was convenient, I told myself. I kept nodding and smiling, even though my face felt coated in a veneer of plaster of Paris that was about to crack.

'She's the sort you start talking to as if you'd only seen her yesterday, so I spent most of my time in Eindhoven with her.'

'Are you going to marry her?'

'What? I'm not even properly divorced.'

'Well, that's some story. You go away and get engaged and I stay here and get married.'

He smiled, but raised his eyebrows.

'Married?'

'Yeah, to a guy Ryan I met up with.' I was trying to joke but it wasn't working. 'Well, not really.'

'Look, Megan. You always said you didn't want a serious relationship.' He spoke calmly but I could see him gripping his right hand with his left, almost pinching it. 'You said you'd get bored, but I want more. I have to think of myself here. It's just so strange – it's like the right person arrived for me at the right moment.'

My noncommittal words flooded back to me. So much for trying to go slow with him, for playing it cool. The irony was I'd just been about to tell him how I felt. All the words I'd rehearsed about moving in together retreated into my head like a whipped dog scurrying down an alley.

'You know I really like you, Megan, but I sat down with my mother and sisters and talked about everything and they all said I should think of my future.'

I was shocked at being discussed like a career choice. I couldn't help imagining his family sitting round the kitchen tucking into stroopwafels and playing Trivial Pursuit and choosing this new woman over me, like choosing new wallpaper.

'So, when are you going back to her?'

'Not yet. I have to hand my notice in to my landlord and boss first.'

'Will you still come here to play with me?'

'Of course, I will.' He moved to the settee to sit beside me. 'You think I told her about you? But I will tell her.' At least he had the grace to look troubled. 'I do care about you a lot, you know,' he said, staring into my eyes.

'I know ... it's funny. I always thought you'd leave me for someone long-term.'

I felt a sob lodged deep in my throat but so far my voice was holding out. He put his fingers through the webbing of mine.

'It's just I don't want to regret not going back to Eindhoven.'

'Life's full of regrets,' I said. 'I even regret my regrets.' You're one of them, I was thinking.

He felt the roughness of my bitten nails with his thumb and playfully pretended to nibble on them. And, if I was another type of woman, I'd have told him to leave, to get the fuck out for cheating on me, but I'd wanted him so much over the past three weeks and I pulled him up from the sofa and up to my bedroom where I kissed him, then jumped on top of him, wanting him deeper than deep in me to take away the pain of his rejection, and I felt his cock hit where my womb joins my abdomen, hurting the muscles, and he pushed me off and grabbed me from behind so that I felt my flesh wave all the way from my buttocks to my stomach to my breasts in one giant tide. All I wanted was to bend my body into impossible and agonizing shapes.

'Ah, your beautiful butt,' he said, stroking it.

'You're beautiful but what?' I retorted, mocking him.

When I gave him a blow job, he lay with his hands behind his back as though I'd tied him up. He moved onto his knees and I aimed for the ridge where the penis meets the foreskin and he had such a look of ecstatic triumph through his slitted sleepy eyes, his arms stretching upwards, that I broke away laughing.

'So, you think that's funny, do you?'

He licked my belly button in punishment as he knew it makes me squirm. He licked me till I quaked before pushing me onto my side, bending my legs like I was a blow-up doll to be manoeuvred for his pleasure. He closed his legs, sliding into me, hitting hard and quick. Then he clambered on top again, diving his tongue in and out of my ear. I clung on to him tight and felt the breadth of his back. It was the most unfettered sex we'd ever had because we both knew it was the last. It was like we were cramming into our mouths every last bit of each other's body.

After he came, I was the first to get up and get dressed. Before I pulled my jeans on, he gave my thighs a couple of gentle smacking kisses as one would to the cheek of a beloved aunt – almost a goodbye kiss.

I had one last question for him.

'If you could go back to being twenty, how would you live your life?'

'That's easy, I'd go wild, party all night. I wouldn't get stuck with a wife and children again. What about you?'

'I wasted all my twenties partying. No, I'd study hard to be a lawyer and have a baby.'

'Oh,' he said.

It was clear we'd always be opposites. I wasn't going to see him again. Once you raised the spectre of the end of a relationship all the fun went out of it. I'd no time for any piquant pangs of sorrow. It was nearly as bad as a cancer diagnosis.

Downstairs I closed my laptop, so I wouldn't be tempted by any more YouTubes. Not that I wanted more catastrophism. Let's face it, I had enough of that from reading Troubles prose. One chapter of 'Milkman' was enough to curdle anyone's milk. No, the only reason I'd watched people falling on film was to imagine how I'd cope with those last seconds myself, to prepare myself for every moment of falling, for every moment like this very one today.

When I thought about things, it all felt ok. I was still pretty young, and pretty and young, and besides, there were plenty more fish at the sushi bar. There's a lid for every pot, as my grandmother used to say. All I had to do the next time I was with a man was be more open, tell him I loved him, I wouldn't hold back. And, after all, if I wanted a kid, I could go to Ryan – avenues were not only open, they were as wide as ever. Sally once told me she wanted the words 'She Kept Going' inscribed on her gravestone, but I was so different and wanted it said of me 'She Went Where No one Else Would Go'. Now I thought about it, I knew I'd never want to be married like Sally. She was so stressed she'd bought a weighted blanket to help her sleep. To be honest, I was almost relieved Aart had ended it.

I went outside, looking at the whin banks on the mountains that were the same electric yellow as the Harland & Wolff cranes. 'Girls is Players Too' was pumping out from the radio of a passing car and, suddenly, I was buzzing with possibilities. I could feel life revving, torquing inside me. The nights were getting lighter and so was I. That was it. The next morning at Trailfinders I'd find my own trail. I'd go to India this July and explore tantric art. And I'd look for a new job, one where I travelled instead of helping others to travel. I was open to everything; freedom was everything. It was my mantra and my tantra. I'd always loved being single.

The Whistleblower

It is the moment Corinne feels like a killer herself. She draws a chair to the bed, looks into the patient's rheumy eyes and says the words, repeated so often they seem now to have a rhythm of their own.

'Unfortunately, your treatment hasn't worked, so we're going to have to get you onto a ventilator. We've already called an ambulance to transfer you to the ICU unit at the Royal.'

'Oh no,' he whispers dysphonically, fright flaring on his forehead.

'You'll be getting the best treatment available.'

She tries to project warmth through her eyes. It's hard to seem human when you're speaking through a mask.

This guy is in his fifties, a little flabby around the midriff, but he has a better chance of survival than most. His muscle mass is good, his skin tissue remarkably resilient and, as is the case in most recoveries from this virus, he shows a keen curiosity in what happens around the ward. Corinne knows more than anyone it's the minute percentages that make the difference.

She asks the nurse to arrange a WhatsApp call between the patient and his wife while she quickly contacts the anaesthetist. Out of the corner of her eye, she notices the ward doctor, Gavin Boyd, assess the patient and scribble in his notepad. Gavin's the figure of fitness in his scrubs, the low beds amplifying his height. He's part of the group her husband Eddie goes cycling with every weekend and sometimes she's unable to dispel an image in her mind of his muscular body in Lycra. It's funny how people call physical attraction 'chemistry', when all it is is biology.

Gavin strides across the ward and hands her the prescription.

'Can you authorise two packs of Cyclimorph?'

'Two?'

'Yes, please. One for the ambulance and one for ICU.'

She knows ICU take care of their own meds, but doesn't have time to object as there are lines to be inserted and oxygen measurements to be taken.

'No problem,' she agrees, rushing back to her patient.

By the time she walks out to the Mater car park at three o'clock, the sun is already starting to sink. She draws in a huge breath of air, feeling the freeze of it in the back of her throat. Her car is parked under a tree and the globules of ice on each twig are gently tapping the bonnet in the wind. It's so fresh out here as if nature is sterilising everything before the healing warmth of spring. She notices for the first time that the frost on the car roof is made up of spiny, frayed, spar-like particles. How did I never notice this before, she asks herself.

She starts up the engine and follows the black wake of wheel marks along the driveway to the Crumlin Road.

'You must be mad,' she says to Eddie.

'Not at all. Sure, even Boydy's doing it.'

'Just because Gavin Boyd's cycling through the Mournes on one of the iciest days of the year doesn't mean it's safe. Doctors are bigger headers than anyone.'

It's bad enough with their children, one of whom is off to Zambia on an environmentalist scheme and the other, at fifteen, harbouring aspirations to be a war correspondent. But Eddie's Benjamin Button routine is starting to really wind her up. Especially as six months ago, he broke his wrist falling from his bike.

'It'll be like cycling down a fucking luge,' she snaps at him.

'Oh, come off it,' he remonstrates. 'Don't exaggerate.'

'I work in a hospital – I'm not going to nurse you at home too.'

She storms out into the bitter air, but the driveway is so crystalline she instantly reverts to baby steps. Winter isn't exactly propitious when it comes to dramatic exits. The beauty and coldness are breathtaking. Opaque hemispheres of ice have formed where rain has spilt from the guttering. She runs the engine while chipping away at the fronds and feathers of frost on the windscreen.

Out on the Lisburn Road, she can see the mountains through the gaps in adjacent streets. There are white rimed paths on the yellow heath of Divis, reminding her of Eddie's Mournes expedition, and she feels a sudden rip of regret at giving him a hard time. Eddie works as an interior designer for offices, formulating clean but functional air-conditioned spaces. No wonder he longs to feel the biting wind and scudding ridges under his wheels. Yet he doesn't appreciate the pressure she's under running the covid ward. Due to recent restructuring, everyone's being funnelled into posts for which they're eminently unsuited.

She parks at the Mater and steps out, carefully avoiding a series of frozen puddles. Orange leaves are trapped beneath them like dried flowers under a pane of glass.

In the ward Ellie, one of the most elderly DNRs, is no longer conscious and her pulse is weak. Corinne listens to her shallow breathing and makes an immediate decision to call her relatives. Timing is everything, as covid rules only allow two family members to come and say goodbye for a brief half hour.

In the next bed Michael seems to be in some distress, complaining of chest pains. It surprises her, given the amount of Cyclimorph Gavin has prescribed.

'Did you administer the Cyclimorph?' she asks the nurse.

'Oh yes. Gavin told me 10 mgs intravenously every four hours.'

'No. It should be 20 mgs,' corrects Corinne, knowing the exact amount she dispensed.

'Well, I only have enough for 10.'

Corinne frowns, wondering where the other pack has got to. Funnily enough, it's been troubling her that the hospital pharmacy can't seem to meet her ward's demands. Gavin's words from the other day about ordering Cyclimorph for the ICU are filtering back to her and she can't help thinking the shortfall is linked to him in some way.

As soon as Gavin starts his shift, she approaches him.

'Do you know anything about some missing Cyclimorph?'

His eyes widen and she wishes she could see his whole face without the mask.

'No. I don't.'

'There's definitely a lack of supplies. You'd almost think someone was pinching it.'

Gavin gives a short laugh. 'Who'd do that? It's hardly ketamine.'

'True.'

'The cleaners must have misplaced it.'

'I suppose,' she says. His words are so matter-of-fact she feels guilty for even thinking it might be him. 'Anyway, Eddie's been telling me about your cycling in the Mournes.'

'Oh, yeah? Well, tell the Edster I've been doing miles on the indoor bike and he'll be eating my dust.'

'Don't you mean your ice particles?'

'Whatever. You just tell him.'

The lightness assuages her worries. Meanwhile, Ellie's daughter and son-in-law arrive and have to be ushered to her bedside. Corinne logs their arrival and just hopes she doesn't have to herd them out while Ellie is in her last gasps. Ellie seems oblivious to them, but at least she can drift away with their loving words in the air around her.

Corinne is administering more Cyclimorph to Michael through his neck line when she hears someone call out.

'I think Mum's just died,' says the woman.

Corinne runs over and confirms that Ellie is dead. She explains to the couple that they can't spend time at Ellie's bedside as she must be zipped up in a bag and taken away as soon as possible.

'Can I leave this crucifix with her?' the daughter asks.

'Of course. I'll see to it.'

It is hard to start detaching the tubes when family members, weeping and distraught, haven't left the ward, but it has to be done and she's grateful for Gavin's help. The mortuary trolley arrives and she signs the paperwork. She is just saying goodbye to Ellie's family when she notices the tiniest but most significant act. Gavin Boyd is slipping one of Ellie's disconnected mainlines into his pocket.

'I'm so happy you had the chance to say goodbye to her,' she says to Ellie's daughter, trying to hide her distraction. Her mouth is saying one thing, but her mind is saying another and it's as though she's almost looking down on herself.

'Thank you for everything you did to make her comfortable,' says the daughter, her face blotched from holding in the tears.

The Mournes are a dark frost-frayed green under the low winter sun. Corinne stands at the foot of the Bloody Bridge waiting for the first of the cyclists to arrive. It's strange to look down into the river and watch the snow-water throw up tumultuous white foam over the boulders when the car park is so icebound and still. Her fingers are starting to turn mauve in the cold.

'Hi, Corinne,' says Béatrice, Gavin Boyd's partner. She opens her car boot to display an extensive array of sandwiches, flasks, and Tupperwares of *tarte au citron*. 'You think we have enough for the boys?'

The boys, goes Corinne in her mocking inner voice, as these men are hardly children, but she gives Béatrice a bye-ball since she's French.

'Enough to choke a donkey, Béatrice,' she says out loud before realising the acerbity of her words and softening them with, 'Looks beautiful.'

Béatrice's chicness in her Astrakhan coat and grey duncher makes Corinne feel preternaturally ordinary in her Parka. Béatrice is beautiful although, if one was to be picky, the end of her nose is a tiny bit short as though God had thought his creation so perfect he'd decided to pack his work in early for the day. Typical of the woman, muses Corinne, to bring a choice of tea – 'hot sweetened Earl

Grey' as well as breakfast tea. What sort of culinary paragon is she? And the sweetening doesn't come from a bog-standard brand of sugar, oh, no, but from the honey produced by her fucking imported Italian bees. The huge wicker basket of sandwiches reminds Corinne of something a *sans-culottes* might use to collect Marie Antoinette's head.

Corinne wanders away, letting the other women chat to Béatrice. It is awkward, monstrous even, to think she's about to destroy Gavin and Béatrice's idyllic life. It also strikes her they are Catholics and might imagine she's doing them down for sectarian reasons. Those kinds of potential nuances are rife in this country.

She'd thought long and hard about reporting Gavin. In the first place, she enjoyed working alongside him and, secondly, he wasn't the only doctor around with a morphine addiction. Besides, it wasn't like she had some puritan embargo on drugs. At university she'd taken the odd toot of coke and numerous tokes of skunk, but she'd always regarded drugs as the playthings of youth to be packed up along with alcoholic benders and promiscuity as soon as real life began. But the issue she could not overlook was the suffering of patients from having their Cyclimorph purloined. She couldn't turn a blind eye as sooner or later another member of staff might report it with the inference that Corinne was complicit. In the end after agonising hours of backtracking, she'd decided to wait until after the Mournes trip rather than subject Eddie to trouble. Gavin Boyd would surely go ballistic at the prospect of losing his whole career in medicine.

There's still no sign of 'the boys' on the road and Corinne begins to worry that Eddie's had an accident. She pokes the toe of her boot at a frozen puddle. A vast archipelago of white ice is mapped in an ocean of black.

Strange fissures of frost make the tarmac look like it's been earthquaked.

Finally, the first cyclist approaches in his fluorescent gilet.

'Go on, baby!' Béatrice is shouting.

This isn't even a race, but Gavin Boyd's legs are pumping up the hill like he's Lance Armstrong, his exposed skin a blooming fuchsia pink in the bitter breeze. It occurs to Corinne that he can't feel the pain, since he is Cyclimorphed to the eyeballs or perhaps one could call it 'cycle-morphed'. She watches Béatrice cover his shoulders in a herringbone blanket and welcome him into her arms.

A minute later, Eddie and the others peddle over the brow of the hill, chapped and shivering. Corinne greets Eddie in relief while Béatrice pours them all a sweetened tea.

'It's made with homemade honey,' Gavin informs Eddie. 'I'm actually allergic to bees and keep asking Béatrice if she's trying to kill me.'

'No, baby. If I wanted to kill you I'd just use the bread knife,' says Béatrice, laughing.

'See what I have to put up with, Corinne?' grins Gavin. 'No wonder I do all that overtime.'

And in that second of bonhomie, Corinne knows it would take a far stronger person than her to bring Gavin down. On Monday morning she will say nothing.

On Sunday night there is a break in the weather. She can feel the rise in temperature as she kicks off her half of the duck-feather duvet. She drifts into a dream where she's transported to heaven, but the queue outside it stretches for miles. An angel with a clipboard asks her what she's done to deserve entrance, but she can't think of a single thing except for helping her patients which she's been paid to do. The queue to heaven is absolute hell to her and she wakes up in a panic in the darkness, the dream lodged in her mind as brightly as a movie trailer.

'What's up?' asks Eddie. 'You've been wriggling round all night.'

It's on the tip of her tongue to confide in him as she always does with work matters, but a sense of Eddie's growing friendship with Gavin silences her.

'Just work,' she says, thumping her pillow flat.

Later, as she arrives at the Mater, her car is buffeted by squalls and the rain starts beating down, throwing a mist of spray onto the flat roof of the covid building. On wild days like this, it's a pleasure to enter the equable climate of the ward. Work, however, is hectic. Five new patients, grey and flailing for air, are wheeled in. Once again she's unaccountably low on morphine. She tries ringing for more supplies, but the line is engaged, so she decides to run down in person.

She stops short on the stairs. A doctor is slumped face-down on the steps below her. From his white-peppered dark hair she can tell it is Gavin.

'Hey!' she calls out, sinking to her knees and moving him into the recovery position.

'Mmm.' Gavin opens his eyes, trying to focus.

'You're ok. You must have passed out there.'

His pupils are spinning back into their central position, his consciousness returning.

'Oh, I'm sorry,' he mumbles.

He tries to get up, but stumbles back onto the metal banisters.

'Take it easy there,' she urges, wedging her body against his to steady him.

'Must have been Saturday's bike ride. Think it took it out of me,' he says, avoiding her gaze.

'Right. Let's get you back to the ward.'

He insists on finishing his shift, ignoring her advice to go home. His swift recovery confirms her suspicions even more. The biggest side-effects of Cyclimorph are dizziness and fainting and it's clear to her now he's not only a danger to himself, but to the whole ward.

As soon as he leaves, she approaches the nurse and asks her to corroborate that phials of Cyclimorph prescribed by Gavin have gone missing. She then makes a call to Joseph, the health and safety manager, and tells him it's an urgent cause for concern.

'Can I ask what it's about?' says Joseph.

'Gavin Boyd,' she says, trying to keep her voice from shaking.

'Come and see me now.'

On her way home, the rush hour traffic is ferocious, so she takes a shortcut through Sandy Row, crawling through narrow streets, the bricks washed by the rain into a muted shade of rust. She can't wait to get home and tell Eddie. He'll have to leave the cycling group but it can't be helped. An inflatable Santa lies flattened in a doorway, with the look of a slumbering homeless man. She passes window boxes of straggling geraniums and red wooden poppies, her eyes alighting on the missing panels of outdoor electricity boxes. One house is draped in icicle-shaped blue lights flashing like an ambulance. She imagines with a shiver what it would be like if she and Eddie had to sell their house and move to this rundown part of town.

On the Lisburn Road she reminds herself that Béatrice is a French teacher at Victoria, and Gavin Boyd will be just fine. The thought strikes her that perhaps Gavin could have a future career as a Sandy Row drug courier, but she dismisses it as unworthily vicious. Still, the problem is beyond her now, passed into other hands. Joseph was suitably shocked and will forward the case to the hospital authorities. From now on, she has to save her empathy for her patients.

Before Christmas, Corinne almost bumps into Gavin in the Mater car park. He crosses her path, striding in his usual preposterously confident manner towards the main entrance, while she pretends to check if her car door is locked. He's already been removed from her ward, so she's astonished to see him. Why would he be back? She'd assumed he was suspended until his misconduct tribunal.

She waits for the sliding doors to swallow him up. Shaken, she heads straight to Joseph's office.

'How can I help you?' Joseph asks with a wary smile.

'I'm confused. I just saw Gavin Boyd come in. I thought after everything I reported ...'

'Look, Corinne, he swears he knows nothing about the Cyclimorph and he was checked for tracks on his arms, his stomach, even his legs, but there aren't any. He isn't injecting.'

'Oh.'

'I have more bad news for you. As far as I know, he's planning to counterclaim against your allegations.'

She can feel her heart click into overdrive. Joseph's hands are loosely interlocked, trying to look relaxed but his thumbs are tapping against each other compulsively.

'But how do you account for his overprescription of Cyclimorph?'

'I agree that it's highly irregular and an example of malpractice. But it isn't enough proof he's self-medicating,' Joseph says with a shrug. 'That's why he's been switched to haematology.'

Back in the ward, she's swept up by the needs of her patients. Michael is coughing in convulsive fits. Corinne quickly fits on the oxygen mask, letting it hiss its kiss of life through his lips.

'You'll be ok,' says Corinne. 'Breathe in more slowly.'

She sits with him a few minutes, holding his hand while adjusting the air pressure.

By the time she arrives home exhausted, Eddie is seated at the dining room table weaving a Christmas wreath out of wintergreen, fir and rosehip branches. She feels a pang to see him holed up indoors instead of training for his next cycling trip.

'They haven't even suspended Gavin,' she tells him. 'All that rigorous questioning I underwent for hours and now he's the one on the attack against me.'

'It'll be ok, love.' He winds a bunch of red berries around the wire. 'He'll slip up sooner or later in the next ward. You did the right thing in protecting your patients.'

It helps to have his calm reasoning. It's more soothing than all the honey-sweetened tea in the world.

'No wonder he was fastest on the bike,' continues Eddie. 'Sure, he didn't even feel the pain. He was the only one of us without gloves. He was bright red all across here.'

He runs his index finger over the knuckles on his left hand. A realisation voltaically runs through her as she recalls a conversation years ago with a nurse working in substance abuse.

'That's it!' she exclaims. 'He's been injecting into the webbing between his fingers – gloves would have irritated the track marks. It's the one place people never look. Thanks, love!'

She gives him a hearty kiss on the cheek.

Michael whose bed is next to the window tilts his head towards her. His breathing is a little less laboured today and his oxygen levels have stabilised. Corinne checks his latest tests.

'The good news is you're covid free,' she tells him.

'Looks like I might make it out of here yet,' he grins.

'No doubt of it.'

He's not out of danger in spite of the encouraging signs, but hope is always the best cure. She sits down by him, surmising his need for company. It's another dark solstitial day and through the window as the invisible sun sets, the clouds turn a gentle indigo. It's as if the hint of colour is a promise, almost a gift, for the new year.

'I keep running over the past,' Michael admits through the hiss and pump of the oxygen tank.

'Better not to,' Corinne smiles.

'Can't help it lying here. Y'know, I once had a really good job in a university library…fifty grand, a pension, set for life.'

'And?'

'A blind student was at the university. I became friends with her, but she couldn't complete her course as the library failed to provide the resources in braille for her. One day, she told me she was going up against the uni in a tribunal and asked for my support. All I had to do was be honest and testify that the library had broken its promise.'

As Michael talks, Corinne thinks of her own story. The news came yesterday that Gavin had been suspended.

'I was in a dilemma,' says Michael. 'Wracked for days, knowing the uni would punish me if I helped her.'

'So what did you do?'

'I remember looking in the mirror before going into the tribunal and it was like the first time I'd really seen myself. I told myself, yes, I could have a house, car, holidays for the rest of my life, but I wouldn't be able to live with myself if I didn't tell the truth. So, I spoke out, she won and I lost my job.'

He lowers his chin in defeat. Corinne pats his hand.

'You did the right thing, Michael.'

'I know,' he nods. 'But ...'

She nods too, understanding that all victories in life are Pyrrhic. After Christmas, she's going to hand her notice in at the Mater and work part time at the Royal. The strains of the ward are too much for her. A sudden shard of red sun lights up the electric green moss on the trees outside.

Michael is coughing convulsively, his hand spreadeagling across his chest.

'Be back in a sec,' she says as she goes to get him his Cyclimorph.

Boglands

'D'you want to see him?' asked Anne.

There was doubt in her face as to why anyone would. She'd kept such a clean house all her life that the coffin in the living room seemed to be an aberration, an anomaly in the domestic order she'd cultivated as assiduously as her husband had cultivated the fields. But she led James to the front room without waiting for an answer, knowing it was custom. The blinds were closed, the electric light rebounding off the polished table.

Brian was zipped up to his chest in silk. He was wearing a light summer suit, the shirt too loose around his neck, the way it was with schoolboys who had yet to grow into their uniforms. James gazed down remembering the big bluff man stomping in from the yard with hands the shade of freshly-dug potatoes, kicking his mud-clagged boots onto the newspaper at the back door. This guy didn't look like his uncle Brian; he was too pale, genteel.

'See? Hardly a wrinkle on him,' said Anne. 'He always said the soft rain here was good for the skin.'

'He looks well on it,' said James, aware of the platitude.

'Aye, it's like he's smiling, isn't it?'

Brian had a tight-lipped smile enlivened with lines of crimson clumsily applied by the funeral home. A half-hearted effort you'd say, but it was definitely a smile. There was a concentrated look on his brow as if death had required his attention. The closed eyelids seemed small and shrunken, at odds with James's memory of large dark eyes. The heavy click of the granddaughter clock in the corner reminded him how loud he'd found it as a child. Now at the age of fifty-six, he could hear the tick of mortality in it too.

'God love him,' pronounced Anne.

James wanted to stay longer with his memories but Anne was already turning away and it didn't do to stand gawping at a dead relative like it was a raree show, so he followed her back through the hall into the light-filled kitchen. The good cups were sitting out in readiness, as was the good teapot though he could see the battered pot she used every day next to the kettle. It seemed poignant somehow.

'Would you take a wee cup of tea?' asked Anne.

He wondered for a second if he should, just to pass himself, but a deep chime came from the clock.

'Jesus, it's like a dinner gong,' he said with a grin. 'That reminds me. I've a farm to inspect.'

At the back door, Anne held his hands tight as she said goodbye to him, conveying her grief without words. He wished he could go to the funeral the next day, but he'd been booked for months to speak at a biosphere conference. As he drove away, the bluebells were shaking under the hawthorn hedge.

A ten-minute drive brought him to the Trassey Road where he felt the lurch of the hillocks in his stomach and shift of the stones under his wheels. The Mournes ahead of him were a mustardy yellow from the whin bushes and the smooth roll of them felt reassuring. The hedges were thinning out into drystone walls. To his left were pine plantations on the steep slopes of Slievenaglogh and, suddenly, the valley opened out into a view of Hare's Gap with its distinctive chink in the wall like a doorway leading up into the sky. The closer he got to the mountains, the craggier they became, torrs jagging above him. Close-up, everything was different.

The road swung away from the mountains. The McGill farm was halfway up a hillside. He hadn't been here for a year since the grant was awarded and the first signs weren't auspicious. The low boggy field seemed trimmed of reeds and long grasses.

He turned in at the open gate, driving up to the house, the dogs racing out to defend their territory. Louise McGill followed them, guldering at them to settle.

'Himself's coming now from the high field,' she said to James. 'Would you come in and wait?'

'Ah, no thanks. I'll just inspect the fields and be off.'

He pulled his wellies out of the 4x4 and changed into them while Louise chatted about the turn in the days and the length of them. He was drawn in by the size of her eyes, the grey flecks in the blue, but at the same time he couldn't help noticing her heavy eyelids. He didn't know whether she was beautiful or ugly. Soon, 'Himself' was heading towards them with the brisk barrelling walk of someone born into the Mournes, the sparse strands of hair flapping on his weathered scalp like duckling feathers in the wind.

'Let's go then,' said Brownlow McGill after a brief bone crusher of a handshake.

They walked down to the low field. The birdsong was muted, but James was relieved to feel the bounce of his feet on the bog-black earth dotted with tiny white specks of granite. There was still the whisper of water from the ditch and, next to it, patches of marsh orchid and shamrock flourished. The bulrushes, however, had disappeared.

'Still mucky as get-out down here, but at least I cleared out that clatter of rushes,' said Brownlow.

The bordering fields were much worse, drier. An outcrop of boulders and blackthorns where swallows had nested had been dug out of the high field.

'You were told to keep the land as it was,' said James.

'Aye, but the Mulhollands called it through-other,' Brownlow explained, nodding in the direction of a neighbouring farm. 'An eyesore they called it.'

When they got back to the driveway, James took a deep breath and spelt out his concerns.

'The way you're going there'll be no more bees, curlews or snipes. Whenever I look at a green field, all I see is an empty desert. You've been paid thousands to keep the bog, not wreck it.'

'Here, you should be thanking me for investing your cash in the land. Most boys'd be splashing out on a luxury cruise or a new set of Turkey teeth. Sure Louise here was begging me to take her somewhere.'

'Wouldn't take me to the door, this boy,' put in Louise.

'Well, I'm afraid I can't sign off the rest of the funding.' James tried to sound firm, but Brownlow was narrowing his eyes.

'What do you want me to do, like?' retorted Brownlow. 'Bring the boulders back on a lorry?'

'No, that's gone, but you can reverse most of what you've done.'

'I can't do this overnight.'

'I'll be back in three months. I'll check on your progress then.'

'So, are you saying we won't get our money till then?' frowned Louise.

'No, sorry. It's the terms of the grant.'

'It'll be the terms of my fucking fist in a second,' growled Brownlow, but Louise grabbed his arm.

'No,' she said, jabbing her finger towards his face to defuse him. 'I don't want any fighting, alright?'

James got into his 4x4 before another word could be said. He could hear his revs as he raced away, catching a glimpse of the dog's bared teeth in the wing mirror. Christ, that couldn't have gone any worse. His hands were shaking on the steering wheel. He passed the dramatic cliffs of Slieve Bearnagh, but hardly took them in. It wasn't that he'd never met an aggressive farmer before. It was inevitable with hundreds of thousands of pounds involved, but he couldn't stop thinking of how one of the other inspectors had had his car windows smashed and his laptop incinerated. With the cost-of-living crisis in full swing, farmers were desperate for grants and digging their heels in harder than ever.

It crossed his mind to go back and sign the forms for McGill for an easy life, but he was angry. Besides, his job wasn't just a job; it was an act of conscience. Getting rid of the bogs had a huge knock-on effect, flooding the villages below, sucking the carbon out of the air. If he let McGill away with it, the other farmers would strip out the boglands, deracinate the rest of the natural world. It would be an eco-disaster.

That night, he had a dream. He was back in his childhood home, sitting on the old floral print sofa next to his sister. Shouts came from the street outside, but he couldn't see what was happening through the closed curtains. He ran over to open them only for Brownlow McGill's furious face to swing up against the window, a crowbar smashing through the glass, scaring the wits out of him. He plunged out of the dream to find himself bound up in his bedclothes, his neck twisted, filmed with sweat.

'Jesus Christ,' he breathed out, rolling onto his back.

He reached out to check his phone. He half thought McGill had sent him an irate text or even a threat, some sort of subliminal message that might have prompted the dream but there was nothing except for a text about the divorce papers from his ex-wife Rachel. He hardly cared about her any more. Funnily enough, she'd always warned him a farmer would get his own back one day.

He went downstairs, not ready to climb down into the steep trenches of more dreams. He opened the front door to hear the dawn birds trilling outside. He didn't have a garden – this terraced house was all he could afford after the divorce – but at least a cherry tree had been planted in the pavement and, as the light came up, its fresh branches were almost raw-red like the skin of a newborn baby.

His thoughts drifted back to how Brian used to greet him by ruffling his hair like he was a farm dog instead of a boy. Brian had been his mother's brother. It was strange how she'd left the family farm to marry a city dweller in Ardoyne. It must have been a shock for a tatie-hoker from the drumlins to end up in a brick row of tiny smokey parlour houses. She'd brought up James in the city, but like her, he didn't belong here. It was like grafting a wild plant to a cultivated one – it just didn't take. He was his mother's son alright.

A wild idea went through his mind of making an offer for the farmhouse. He suspected Annie wanted to move in with her son, Mark, who had no interest in farming and would maybe give him a good price to keep the farm in the family. A picture suddenly formed of his own bogland in that peaty field over the back hill, the shining water on it, and he'd grow mosses, cranberries and pickerelweeds for the bees to graze on. Oh, maybe the concept was mad, but he'd easily get his own grant since he could fill in those forms with his eyes closed. If he saved up every month and kept his old 4x4 on the go, he could surely build up a nest egg to do it. You can take the boy out of the country, his mother had said, but you can't take the country out of the boy. The drumlins would always be in him like a blood blister just under the skin.

A few days later, he returned to the house he was born in. He'd been three years old when they'd left Ardoyne and had never been back since. He hadn't seen the point before as his mother rarely talked of it while she was alive. It was the culture back then not to talk of what happened during the Troubles. This was partly due to Protestant stoicism, and partly just to be different from the Catholics who immortalized their own evictions to win the approval of the international media. But now he couldn't stop thinking about that dream and the street, the shape of the windows, and he didn't know if these visions were real or implanted by his mother. Perhaps they were some sort of bitter seeds that had grown into something surreal.

After work, he headed north beneath the brown-saddled backs of the Belfast mountains. The roofs of the houses were like tiled steps going up the slopes. He parked some streets away from Farringdon Gardens to get a sense of the place, then scuffed through fallen blossom as brown as wood shavings and past a chapel boasting an alabaster Jesus in its grounds with the physique of a body builder. You'd think Jesus was on a protein shake diet, he laughed to himself, then worried he was being sectarian. Some man was heading towards him, so drunk his eyes were flying around like pinballs, and James had to body swerve him.

It was number seventeen, his mother had told him. It looked smart, white-silled, the brickwork clean. The windows were large, though he recalled a lack of light in the house. Perhaps it was a false memory inspired by his mother's account of that week in August when she'd said the windows were boarded up and a mattress shoved against the front door. According to her, he was outside playing as men with burning torches came down the street. His only definite recollections were of fleeing with his mother, father and sister through the back door with their belongings in pillowcases and of sleeping on the floor of a local school. They moved into a prefab home for a while, and whenever his father asked his mother if there was any chance of a council house, she'd lie, pretending there were none on offer, holding on to her dream of returning to Ardoyne. In the end, the family went to Ballysillan.

Ten years after being burnt out, James's sister left for England, sick of the violence, and never returned. 'We didn't just lose a house, we lost a daughter,' his mother once said, making James feel dutybound to stay in Belfast. Some people thought it was strange that a city boy studied land management, but it was true that half of Belfast in those days was one generation from the farm. Looking back, it made sense for him to study the land when his own family was evicted from it.

The effects, though, of Ardoyne had cut deeper than he'd realised. For the rest of her days, his mother always kept the back door open. She told people she was claustrophobic, but James knew the real reason.

A shadowy figure swung into view at the front window, a pair of eyes peering out. James moved away. There was no point haunting the place, but he was glad to put an image to his family trauma. He turned the corner past an entry full of torn bags and detritus, revealing the roughness behind the gentrification. By the bins, a black and white cat padded up to a ginger cat and attacked it with a howl. They were in a deathroll, biting one another in a ball of teeth and frenzy. James shouted out and kicked at the gate beside them, but they ignored him. There was nothing to do but leave them to it. A middle-aged man outside the pub ditched his fag and ran across to film it with his phone.

'Fight, you fuckers, fight!' he yelled.

By the time James made it home across the city, it was late. The sky was branded with a big red ball of sun, its perimeter ashen with clouds. As the light sank behind the mountains, one last grey postmark of a cloud sent the day on its way.

In August he was ready to revisit Brownlow McGill's farm. There had been no communication whatsoever in the past three months, even though he'd sent McGill a booklet on preserving bogland. On phoning Louise to arrange a meeting, she'd been terse with him, but had agreed on a date.

He called in at Brian's farm on the way. It seemed strange to call it Anne's farm now, but when he arrived, there she was standing strong as a tree in the doorway. Her muddy boots and a bucket of potatoes were in the porch, signaling that the old traditions continued.

'You're looking grand on it,' he told her.

'Ach, Mark comes round every day. He's awful good to me.'

'Now, I wouldn't want to be stepping on any toes, but here goes,' he said, launching into his plans for the farm if he bought it one day.

'Uh huh,' she kept nodding, tilting her head to one side, then to the other as she weighed up how her son and grandchildren could benefit.

At the end of it, she smiled. 'Who'd have thought progress would look like wilderness? How and ever, Brian would have loved you to have the farm. You know, he wanted all of you to come here after you were put out.'

'I never heard that.'

'Oh, aye, but your mum had this notion you children would have better futures in the city. She only stayed there for you, you know.'

Anne promised to talk things over with Mark as they moseyed out to the yard. The cows were in a nearby field flicking their tails at the flies like portly grandes dames wafting their fans at a garden party.

'By the way, do you know the McGills?' he asked.

'Oh, aye, they worship at Kilmegan like us. Brian would have had some dealings with them,' she said, giving away nothing.

As he left in his 4x4, the fuchsia hedges were jigging in the breeze and the cow parsley was frothing in the sheughs. The idea of going back to his mother's land was thrilling him and not even the prospect of Brownlow McGill's hard-chaw face could blemish it. Turning onto the Bryansford Road, he could see the fields beneath the Mournes tussocked and clumped with stretches of cracked black peat, just a faint cloud or two smoking across the slabs of Bearnagh. He loved this part of the world. When he thought now of the divorce from Rachel, it seemed the best thing that could have happened to him. Rachel was an avowed city girl, heading out for her Prosecco nights with her mates. Sometimes she'd laughed with James at how the girls affected an urban coolness, toasting each other with '*Sláinte*, motherfuckers!', but mostly she was happy to be one of them. In the beginning, she'd liked driving out to nature with him, but always chose the manicured arboretum of Castlewellan, the pink rose gardens of Lady Dixon Park over the wilderness. It was astonishing to think they'd lasted ten years; they had never been fully right for each other, never quite fit. They were like two boulders in a drystone wall where the wind whistled through. She liked the feel of her step on concrete, whereas he preferred the soft jelly quiver of an ancient bog, that feeling of defying gravity. For a while, he'd worried that his heart had been smashed apart by her, but it was just weathered, holed but intact, like a limestone rock.

He wasn't able to park in the McGills' driveway. It was being retarmacked by some slovenly workmen who were sitting slumped on the wall enjoying a fag. He revved onto the thick grass at the side of the road and walked up through the garden, nodding a hello to the workmen who gave the lightest tilt of their heads back. Already he noticed there were no new bulrushes in the low field, but it didn't surprise him. Brownlow McGill was too thrawn to ever admit he was wrong.

Brownlow had spotted him and was striding towards him.

'Right, let's take a look,' said James, trying to muster some positivity.

'It's looking rightly,' insisted Brownlow. 'I've improved it no end. The bog bilberry and the bedstraw's taking hold as you'll see.'

Down in the fields, the earth felt spongier underfoot and a lapwing swooped down on the laterals overhead. The remaining boulders were still there, decorated with lichen, but much more was needed.

'I'll write you a five-point action plan before I leave,' said James, once they'd walked back to the house.

'What about the money?' Brownlow asked, his hair flicking up, aggravated by the breeze.

James hesitated. He couldn't be viewed as a soft touch, yet he was prepared to meet them halfway. He could see Louise marching out of the back door to join them.

'I can release half of it this month, but the rest will be dependent on future action.'

'But I already took action.' A bit of spittle flecked out of Brownlow's mouth. 'I knew you wouldn't play fair. He won't play fair at all, Louise.'

'Here, what sort of a damp hole of a place do you expect us to live in?' added Louise, 'Even as it is, everyone's laughing at us, calling us the bogtrotters.'

James was aware of the tarmackers tuning into every word.

'Sure, the reason we need the driveway done is because it's all subsiding into the bog,' raged Brownlow. 'Who's going to pay for that, Mr Eco-Freak?'

'You're getting half the money, aren't you?' continued James. 'I'm being as generous as I can.'

Something was wrong. Louise was looking past him, distracted, and he smelt a burning in the air. He turned to see the flicker of orange flames through the spindly hedge.

'Oh Jesus, no!' he shouted and started running down the garden towards his 4x4. The fumes of petrol filled his nostrils. The fire had already taken hold and it would only be a matter of time before the engine blew, but he had work files in the boot and yanked it open to rescue them, praying he wouldn't get caught in the explosion. He hauled them out, then ran to the edge of McGill's driveway.

Brownlow and Louise were still standing by the house, staring down at him. The tarmackers were loitering round the cement mixer, looking guiltily away as they pretended to get on with the job. It crossed his mind that parked on a quiet country road, he'd never be able to prove that Brownlow McGill was behind it. He had so many enemies. He looked back at his 4x4, listening to the roar of the flames, the sound stirring something deep in his memory. Beneath his feet, came the quiet trickle of the bog as it wended its way down the valley.

Waiting at Milltown

On the morning of the burial, the wake was still in full swing. Sixty shades of soup were on the go in the kitchen. Sandwiches were lined up on a plate like the bellows of an accordion.

'Is there no drink?' asked one of the new arrivals.

'Tea, coffee or glue,' joked Roisin's son Dermie. 'Pick your poison.'

There wasn't a chance Roisin was offering drink. If you did, you'd get all the undesirables of the district rocking up for a swall, folk who'd never heard tell of Stella McFerran or would malign her while she was still warm in her coffin. Besides, she didn't want Dermie falling off the wagon, although he seemed in good form today, ladling out portions of pasta and heating them up in the microwave.

'It's Irish carbonara or, as I call it, McCarbonara,' he grinned. 'And watch out or it'll burn the bake off you.'

Roisin was making coffee when Dermie took her to one side.

'The peelers are at the end of the street,' he whispered into her ear, so close she squirmed from his breath. 'Special Branch.'

She threaded her way between neighbours chatting in her hallway and past the smokers standing in the gazebo Dermie had set up to accommodate them. Over the three days of the wake there had been a fair pelt of rain but the blue had broken through at last.

Yet another mourner was opening her gate – it was like a turnstile at Glastonbury! It was all a friend of a friend of a friend and it was strange how people flocked to see republican royalty. This man looked vaguely familiar as many older men did in west Belfast, making her wonder if he'd been in one of the recent Troubles documentaries churned out on the BBC.

'Very sorry for your trouble,' he muttered, avoiding her eyes. He gave her a double handshake to reinforce his sympathy.

'Thanks. Go on in and help yourself to a drop of soup and some cake,' she answered, making a mental note not to keep mentioning the soup as if it was more important than her aunt's demise. For all she knew, the man could have been Stella's lover. Or cell commander.

She took a couple of tokes from her vape, looking up the slope of the road and, sure enough, about twenty metres away two shadowy heads were peering out of the depths of an unmarked car. She stared hard to let them know she'd spotted them. Decades after the peace process the State still haunted her family. Who d'you think we are, the New IRA, she longed to call out. The smatter of republicans who had visited to pay their respects hadn't handled a gun in years. Police intimidation pure and simple it was, as well as punishment for the past.

The hearse rolled over the brow of the hill and a frisson of panic butterflied through her chest. She gave the funeral director a brief wave and hurried back inside.

'Dermie, Thomas is here,' she called.

Dermie was standing by the open coffin in the living room, taking a last look at Stella. Relatives and friends behind him were chatting lightly about their new sofas and foreign holidays, talking about cash and the price of things, never thinking that the cost of life was always death. You paid up in the end for the privilege of living and even more so for the privilege of taking a life.

Her aunt was small in her coffin, the lines in her face deep. She'd only been sixty-nine and her final years had been racked with rheumatism and addiction to painkillers which didn't mean her pain was psychosomatic, but even so, there had been acceptance in her eyes, an embracement of her illness as the natural course of things.

'At least she's at peace,' said Dermie, a wistfulness imbuing his words.

Roisin glanced sharply at him.

'Oblivion's no answer,' she replied, hearing her own curtness. 'Thomas is here.'

'No worries,' said Dermie, taking a photo down from the mantelpiece.

It was an image of the young Stella in combats and a beret, holding an AK-47. Portrait of a young female as a freedom fighter, thought Roisin, noting Stella's compressed lips and wide-open impassioned eyes. Dermie tried to tuck the photo between Stella's intertwined fingers, but it was tricky as rheumatism had enlarged the knuckles and misshapen the bone. The funeral parlour had given Stella long pink waxy fingernails that only accentuated the flaw. Madame Tussaud's finest, Roisin had joked with Dermie when the coffin first arrived.

Roisin headed back into the hall to greet Thomas. He was sporting a black three-piece suit and pocket watch that wouldn't have looked out of place on some lugubrious character in a Dickens novel.

'Sorry again for your loss,' Thomas said, head bowed. 'We'll take her now.'

His sons, Patrick and Finbar, were wheeling in the metal bier. It was all so formal – no Tommys, Paddys or Fins to be had in the funeral business. The laughter from the gazebo had died away.

It took Patrick and Finbar a while to screw down the lid.

'Aye, lads, make sure she doesn't get out,' some wag was whispering in the hallway.

Patrick tried to suppress a smile when somebody's phone played a rave anthem.

'God rest her soul,' murmured Roisin, though she didn't know why she said those words. The woman wouldn't have had a priest next nor near her while she was alive. The march of Marxism had had precious little truck with the will of God. Still, she felt suffused with softness and the words 'Róisín Dubh' kept playing in her mind as it was the soubriquet Stella had given her as a child. It struck her painfully, though, that she'd never done anything for Ireland except for tending to Stella in the last weeks of her life, but that was done out of blood loyalty, not out of any empathy for her aunt's patriotic crusade.

Dermie stepped forward with the man she'd met at the gate. As they silently draped an Irish tricolour over the coffin, she realised exactly who it was – Sean Moynihan, a local republican dissident. Wasn't he the one involved with the Abbie Convery disappearance all those years ago? She felt a surge of anger at Dermie inviting Sean without even consulting her, and Stella certainly hadn't made any request for him to be there, but it was too late to do anything about it now. She'd warned Dermie to keep the political angle down to a minimum in case they all appeared in the papers, but he hadn't a titter of wit, the same boy.

The coffin was topped with a bouquet of arum lilies and everyone followed it into the street, except for Roisin's cousins who were frantically tinfoiling the remaining sandwiches. Roisin had washed her car but she still found it old and scruffy, unbefitting for the day it was. She watched through her rear view mirror the Special Branch pull away, feeling a sense of relief. Funnily enough, she'd imagined this day for years, envisioning men and women in balaclavas shooting into the air, but Stella had long since sacrificed that honour by revealing too many of her deeds in interviews. IRA threats had forced Stella to move house across the border where she'd stayed for the last decade of her life. Before she died, she'd asked Roisin to wake her in Turf Lodge.

'Ah, the notion of being home again,' Stella had said, her eyes lighting up one last time before she ran out of the spirit to keep them open.

Roisin noticed the faintest quiver of the wind on the lilies as the coffin disappeared into the back of the hearse and it brought the first tears of the day to her eyes, just that idea of the fragility of a woman, of a great republican warrior, and how the past still echoed through this city. A thought came into her head of an unmarked grave on some farmland, but she immediately suppressed it.

Dermie got in beside her while a cousin and Dermie's friend, Kevin, barrelled into the back.

'Isn't it a great day?' said her cousin, implying that the sun was a God-given blessing on their family. 'Especially after all that thunder we've been having.'

It was a long drive down the mountainside and across the city to the rolling Castlereagh Hills. A huge convoy of cars crawled behind the hearse. It was impressive, thought

Roisin, that a woman who had no children was worthy of such a send-off.

'I've a mate,' Kevin piped up from the back, 'who says they burn fat people at night, so you don't see all the smoke off them.'

'Good joke, Kev,' Dermie said, laughing loudly.

'It isn't a joke.'

Half an hour later, Roisin was bristling.

'What do you mean there's no cremation?'

'I'm very sorry,' insisted the registrar, a dumpy kindly woman, 'but our records say you booked a burial. And even if we could change it, the crematorium is always closed on Saturdays.'

Roisin swivelled round to meet Dermie's eye.

'It's a total fuck-up. I'm so sorry, Mum,' he moaned. 'I thought I'd ticked cremation.'

'The one thing I asked you to do!'

'You have two choices,' said the registrar. 'Either go ahead with the burial now as the plot's ready for you or wait for a cremation in three days' time.'

'I can't take her home with me,' said Roisin, the horror rising. 'I couldn't take another three days of wake.'

'Besides, everyone's here,' added Dermie. 'They'll go buckmad if we ask them to come back on Tuesday.'

'We'll go for it then.'

'What Stella doesn't know won't hurt her,' agreed Dermie.

Guilt forked like lightning through Roisin as she signed the forms. She'd seen fear flit across Stella's face at the very mention of a burial. And it seemed plain wrong to bury her here in these tame placid grounds instead of Milltown

Cemetery at the foot of her beloved mountains, but it couldn't be helped.

Dermie gathered the group of mourners outside the crematorium to make his announcement. 'I'm sorry, everyone. There's been a change of plan. Stella is to be buried with a graveside service if you'll follow Mum to the plot.'

'Lost the plot, you mean,' someone muttered with a chuckle.

Thomas was unperturbed. 'Not a problem,' he reassured Roisin. 'Happens all the time and it's a grand day for a graveside ceremony.'

She could hear Kevin tell Dermie, 'You total fucking ballbag, it'll cost you a packet for a gravestone.'

Roisin made her way over to the priest, a distant relative whom she'd already roped into saying some words about Stella out of form's sake. She couldn't help feeling like a character in a black farce as she apologised for the mix-up, ushering him over to the dug-out square surrounded by sand-pale earth. She watched Dermie, her cousins and Sean Moynihan lift the coffin from the back of the hearse. It seemed a decent spot to be buried, a sun trap with the shade of the beeches casting oval shadows across the gravel path. Wild roses were growing around a nearby grave, shaking their peppery stamens.

She stood at the front of the crowd, unable to take her eyes off Dermie, noticing the blackness of his tattoos against the white collar of his shirt. His hair which was long on top was shaved down one side. She hated his new hairstyle as she reckoned he looked like a patient about to undergo brain surgery. Of course, she couldn't tell him that as he was doing so well now she didn't want to upset him, but she should never have given him the responsibility of booking the funeral. He'd had relapses before and, at twenty-five, was a long way from 'getting his shit together' as he called it. There was a sticky sickly sheen of sweat on his face like the honeydew on the leaves of the nearby sycamores and it worried her.

Even worse, a local journalist was watching the funeral from afar, no doubt noting with vindictive pleasure that Sean Moynihan was carrying the coffin.

It was the day after the funeral and there was a mountain of dishes to be washed on the sideboard. The kitchen window looked out onto the heathered slopes. She could see the spindly blackthorn where Stella used to hide guns, knowing no one, not even the Brits, would search there for fear of being cursed by the fairies. Above Divis, light cuttlefish bones of cloud were floating in the blue pool of the sky.

'Do you think it's true that extremism can be passed down from generation to generation?' Dermie asked, as he dried the soup bowls.

'Nonsense. If you're talking about Stella, she was just a product of her time. She was radicalised young.'

'I've never got over what she did.'

The papers had been full of Abbie Convery's disappearance since Stella's death. On the night of the abduction, Stella had been the one to drive Convery away from the Falls, pretending that the IRA were relocating her to a Sisters of Mercy refuge for her own safety. At the border near Newry, Stella had stopped at a farm. She told Convery to help dig a hole in the ground to bury some weapons, but it was just a ruse to get Convery to remove her wedding and engagement rings. Stella led her into an outhouse where a comrade shot her in the head. Convery's children received the rings the next morning.

'Stella gave that woman fags, a cup of tea from a flask, knowing she was taking her to her death,' said Dermie.

'I know, but she was convinced at the time that Convery was an informer and, anyway, the Converys were bad news, burgling all around them. Everyone in the district wanted rid of them.'

She thought back to Stella's last days when the pneumonia was in her lungs. It had been on the tip of Roisin's tongue to say something to comfort her, to acknowledge the leading part she'd played in the conflict while other women had sat on their soft-furnished arses at home, but something stopped her, an idea that she wasn't worthy of conferring forgiveness. She was frightened of churning trouble up in Stella's mind or even worse of having her words dismissed. Stella's shallow rhythmical breathing soon became as slow as rain dripping off a leaf and it was a peaceful end after a war-scarred life.

'I love you,' Roisin had called out to Stella as soon as the breathing had stopped. She kept calling it again and again, wishing she'd been able to say it more in life.

Looking back, she should have asked Stella about that night. Oh sure, Roisin had been brought up in a republican family that had justified Stella's actions, as she was now doing with her own son, but knowing so little about that one night had always made her feel unsettled and inconsequential, as if viewing something beyond her knowledge or surveying the dark matter, stars and dust of the universe from afar. There was a famous quote about the past being a foreign country, but to her the past had always been a distant galaxy.

She still wondered if there was a genetic connection between Stella's addiction and Dermie's. Oh, she knew everyone talked of transgenerational trauma these days, but most people used it as an excuse with which to exonerate their children's bad behaviour. Dermie had started smoking dope after school and graduated to the strange cocktails of sleepers, epilepsy drugs and antidepressants circulating the streets of Turf Lodge. Dermie had later been diagnosed with permanent psychosis, but Roisin told him not to believe it, just as she'd refused to believe the hole in his heart as a baby would limit his life to a few years.

'You were my miracle baby,' she told him. 'You still are.'

Over the months after Stella's death, Dermie stayed sober. He took a job with a mate who ran a dog-grooming business, and came back every day with amusing stories about manicuring an angry chihuahua or applying a blueberry face mask to a growling Doberman.

Roisin was glad to see him laugh. They also ribbed each other about the fiasco of Stella's funeral.

'Don't worry, Mum, I'll make sure you get cremated even if I have to put you in a pizza oven myself.'

'Don't you dare,' she replied with a grin.

When he suggested moving into Kevin's flat on the Falls, Roisin, however, wasn't fully convinced.

'Sure Kevin's responsible. He works as a carer,' Dermie pointed out.

'Oh, come off it, the lad can't even look after himself never mind you.'

She was wary of Dermie having a relapse out of her sight, but had to accept it was time for him to branch out on his own.

The temperature plummeted in the middle of November. On these clear nights the sun set behind the black smooth disc of Divis, leaving a corona so bright it looked like an eclipse.

November was always a busy month for Roisin in the marketing department of An Cultúrlann. She was up to her oxters in Christmas press releases and social media posts, but sometimes when the sun shone through the

Cultúrlann's stained-glass windows, it reminded her that it was once a Presbyterian church. History had a way of catching up with you in this city; it was in the bricks and glass as well as the bones of the living. She didn't admit it to Dermie, but she still fell prey to the occasional attack of guilt over Stella's burial and couldn't help thinking of Stella's fanaticism spreading through the earth like a canker, leaving some dark residue in the soil. It would have been more fitting for a mind that had burnt with so much internecine rage to meet with its own fiery end; it would have been better if her ashes had blown away from these streets forever.

When Roisin's phone rang at twenty to midnight, she grabbed at it, scared that it was news about Dermie. No one would ring at this hour unless it was bad news.

'Hi Mum. Kevin is missing.'

She was relieved to hear Dermie's voice. He told her he'd been watching TV the previous night when Kevin had left their flat. It wasn't unheard of for Kevin to disappear on a bender, but he hadn't returned all day and wasn't responding to phone calls. Dermie had contacted every mutual friend he could think of and there was still no word of Kevin.

'Phone the police now,' urged Roisin.

After she rang off, she couldn't sleep. She went downstairs and stood vaping at her front door. A frosty fog was snooding the mountain and, each time she exhaled, a huge plume of her own white breath jetted out. The sheer volume of breath in her lungs surprised her, filled her with a sense of the immensity of being alive, a sense of gratitude even.

The next day, Kevin's disappearance was all over the local news. CCTV footage showed him walking in the dark past the Red Devil Bar in his good wool coat, best suit and Oxfords. He was filmed for two miles, but the footage stopped near Milltown Cemetery. His estranged mother in Cork made an appeal for people with any information to step forward, before the coverage cut to a clip of the police searching the cemetery.

'Jesus, the peelers wouldn't have dared set a foot in Milltown in the past,' Roisin said to Dermie.

'He's dead, I know it,' said Dermie, a lone tear tracking down his cheek.

'Look, love, until Kevin's found, there's still hope.'

The news ended with the police saying they had no reason to expect foul play.

A mild wind was heralding the return of the rain when Roisin and Dermie drove through the yellowy grey sandstone gates of Milltown Cemetery. On both sides, Celtic crosses were standing tall and, to Roisin's eyes, they looked like a hundred crosshairs trained on the south and east of the city that lay below. She parked beside the republican plot. It occurred to her that the last time she'd been to Milltown was as a child one Easter Sunday with her mother and Stella. Back then, tricolours had beaten back and forth on their poles but it was quiet now except for the gentle swish of leaves and the scrape of a rake on a gravelled grave. Dermie pointed out where Kevin's uncle was buried. 'A proud volunteer' it said on his headstone.

'He died in a bomb attack, I think,' Dermie said, shrugging.

A taxi driver nearby was showing two American tourists a roll of honour and regaling them with stories of the hunger strikers. 'A plot here would cost you an arm and a leg *and* a shoulder,' he was telling them. 'Nine grand or more.'

'Did you hear that?' she whispered to Dermie and it made her feel better knowing she could never have afforded a republican burial for Stella.

She and Dermie stopped a few seconds to take in the view of the Castlereagh Hills panning round to the twin spires of St Peter's before they took the path down the slope past the poor ground. They passed cross after cross threaded with giant rosary beads. The sun was trying to burst through the achromatic clouds, but kept aborting its mission. The taxi sped past them.

'Typical Americans,' said Roisin, 'doing Belfast in five minutes.'

'Aye. Fast food trauma tourism alright!' joked Dermie.

She headed with Dermie down to the thick undergrowth and trees by Bog Meadows. She'd only agreed to take him here as he'd been fretting in his flat. It was now three days since Kevin had gone missing and the police search had proved fruitless. She and Dermie both suspected the police had been remiss – after all, they wouldn't be keen on staying long in a famously republican cemetery.

They passed the infants' graveyard with its small heart-shaped stones and angel motifs.

'An angel born asleep,' read Roisin from an inscription, but Dermie wasn't listening and bounded into the thick grass and red ferns wet from where the frost had melted overnight. She suddenly remembered this landscape from the footage of a notorious attack on an IRA funeral. She'd only been a young child at the time, but it had always made her shiver.

'There's a river just here,' said Dermie, crashing on through the brambles and dead thistles, scanning the bushes for Kevin. The last of the chestnut leaves had black spots like they'd been scorched by cigarette ends.

'Careful you don't slip into the water!'

His voice shouted out to her, 'No way through here. It's all fenced off.'

They walked back to the path together. White Marian statues seemed to be hovering above a sea of tombstones, the mountains looming behind. Roisin recognised the names of families she'd known growing up. The oldest graves were toppled and tilted by tree roots and devoured by ivy; one Celtic cross was tangled with briars like a witch's hair. Roisin remembered being with Stella on that Easter Day and confiding in her about the bullying she suffered at school.

'Bully them back,' Stella had advised. 'Keep your elbows sharpened, girl.'

It was strange how it took being in a cemetery for the words of the dead to come back to her. She felt so close to Dermie. She was beginning to think they should have more days out, maybe next time to the top of Black Mountain. She pointed out an ivy-festooned tree trunk that was wreathed with red fabric roses.

'Isn't it beautiful?'

There was a gap in the hedge onto a dirt road.

'Let's have one final check,' suggested Dermie.

The ravine was steep-edged around the bouldered river.

Trees had already slipped down the gorge and their torsos obscured the view. Roisin wandered downstream till her eye picked out something odd through a veil of bare branches. She stopped mid-step. Five metres below, she could see a figure in a black coat lying in the water, bobbing gently. The dead leaves of a copper beech were rustling as the chill of the river ran over her heart. His face was pale and half-submerged, but it was Kevin. She knew instinctively that he must have lain down in the meltwater on that icy night and let the coldness take him.

'Nothing here!' called Dermie, making her stir.

'Nothing here either,' she replied, walking towards him briskly.

She'd already decided. She wasn't going to let Dermie be haunted by Kevin's image all his life. There were enough images in his mind of the Convery murder and from now on the only dead for him would be buried under the earth.

'Let's go back to the car.'

On the way to the Falls, she told him about the Troubles and how the Brits used to spread rumours that the cemeteries of west Belfast were haunted. It meant that they could set up their surveillance equipment behind the gravestones at night unimpeded.

'Crafty bastards,' said Dermie, grinning.

The only thing that mattered to her was protecting her son. Once she'd left Dermie back at his flat, she would phone the police. There were times in life you had to let bodies lie in peace. Kevin would just have to lie there a while longer.

All About Erin

Her name was Erin Campbell. And believe me, it was calculated because on her very first application for arts funding, she used her real name – the more prosaic Ellen Campbell which failed to open the doors she craved. Erin Campbell on the other hand was a perfect fusion of Irish and Scottish. It was a name to appeal to both sides in Ireland in spite of her Protestant religion. She changed her name to Erin Campbell and from the day we met I had a problem with her.

Are you thinking I had a problem just because she was a better writer than me? No, it was because she was an expert in artifice. She was assiduous in making connections. One day, an email arrived in my inbox requesting a meet-up. Knowing she was on a charm offensive and that every half-decent writer in Belfast was in receipt of the same missive, I made up some excuse about being away in England. I knew about her, of course, long before I met her. There were the photos of her in all the papers with long black hair, sometimes straightened, sometimes carefully teased into nonchalant waves and there was often the edge of a tattoo creeping onto her neckline, just to temper her well-groomed façade with a down-widda-kidz vibe. She had a boho taste in earrings and once appeared wearing a torc like a Celtic queen.

I'm not into clothes at all, but I'd say her style was alternative yet establishment – an eclectic mix of suede boots, tailored jackets and shiny silk dresses matched with the occasional grungy tear of denim. She was never pastel – her colours were bold – and, yes, I'm realising I sound obsessed, but truly she did fascinate me. I was the total opposite; I had a wardrobe of identical clothes like Einstein – a series of black polo necks, black or blue jeans and a few pastel linen shirts. I had blond hair I repeatedly asked hairdressers to shape, but they never quite managed to make it look anything other than short. It seemed whatever I said, I lacked the conviction to make them think I deserved a style. I don't want to imply I wasn't attractive. I had great bone structure that my somewhat rudimentary understanding of makeup couldn't efface. Men, in general, loved me and sometimes women too. I just wasn't sure I had a discernible style, though Erin once said of a black wool coat of mine, 'That's a great look for you.' Perhaps some of us do find our style, only we just don't see it. It was definitely my style, however, to save my style for the page. It was my style to rip the arse out of the word 'style' – ok, I'm completely joking now which was really my style. What I mean to say is that if Erin had the image, I had the substance.

Before Erin Campbell came along, I'd been coining it in for ten years and flaunting my reputation for being acerbically outspoken. A decade is a veritable epoch in the ephemeral world of publishing and I'd long since morphed from emerging writer into literary powerhouse. But post-Erin, I was losing money and gigs hand over fist. I'd started my writing career the traditional way by actually writing which one might think was a prerequisite, but Erin was different, part of the new breed. She began by being a mentor to other writers, running creative writing groups, curating festivals, reviewing, blogging, doing a Ph.D. in literature ... the writing came second. I avoided these sideshows, but should have noticed much earlier the value in training future acolytes. By the time I did, Erin Campbell had permeated Belfast's literary scene, and yes, permeate was the word for it because she was ubiquitous.

Looking back objectively, some kind of Erin Campbell was always bound to disturb my cosy cocoon. My slide was inevitable and I couldn't blame her for that. I'd ridden the arse off my slice of luck for a long time. Other writers had muscled in to my sphere, but most found it too mentally tough to hang around and moved within a few years into easier genres like journalism or even, poor bastards, into the obscure but well-funded realms of Ulster-Scots poetry. In a city like London, Erin Campbell and I could have coexisted in total harmony, barely registering on each other's radar. In the pond of Belfast, though, there wasn't enough room for two big fish, especially if one was a piranha (I'll leave you to guess which). My major disadvantage was being eleven years older than Erin Campbell's tender twenty-nine, for literary circles venerated youth, as did the whole neophile world of publishing. Sometimes I thought she looked older and she may well have edited her birth date along with her name. And why not? I've always said that writers' greatest works of fiction are themselves. I've lied a shedload about the literary prizes I've won.

One day, I noticed her name as winner of the lucrative *Guardian* Short Story Prize. I read the first paragraph and left it at that. It was enough to tell me she had talent. I also spotted her setting up a literary fundraiser for some fashionable political cause and, not long after, I finally met her at a book launch at the John Hewitt. I was late as usual, flitting by to show my face. My publisher often urged me to go to these things to have 'meaningful chats', but I'd always been more into meaningless hook-ups and scarfing the free drink. As I scooped up a glass of red wine, Erin Campbell strolled towards me.

'You're Adele!' she exclaimed with a huge smile.

'Yep and you're Erin.'

I recognised her immediately from her media headshots. In person, she was tall, willowy and engaging.

'Oh, I should get some wine too,' she said. 'I don't really drink it, but it always looks good holding a glass in public.'

I gave a little internal raise of the eyebrows.

'By the way, your short stories are amazing,' she continued.

'Thanks. I'm still writing them, but I've just started work on a novel.'

'Sounds great. I'm running a small group for writers to engage with each other's work. Do you already have someone who reads you?'

'Apart from my publisher, no.'

'So why don't you join my group then? We also discuss the books of contemporary greats.'

'No way,' I said, shocked that she expected me to join her vanity project. 'I'm not giving my stuff to people I don't trust.'

'But if you don't get feedback, how will you ever improve?' she said, irritated. 'Surely you want to get better. I know I do.'

I mumbled something noncommittal. I was happy with what I wrote, but to say so seemed crass and boastful. Deep down, I was furious. I'd learnt to write experientially and there was no chance I was joining some soppy writers' group, as the wrong feedback could destroy your work. Besides, having to read the poor fiction of wannabes would, if anything, have an adverse effect on mine, plus I was at a different place in my career than Erin and no matter what way she cut it, she was ridiculously reducing me to her level. All these thoughts and more were passing through my head. I could have said them out loud, but there was no way I was revealing my superiority complex and I wasn't going to risk showing her how to be a real author in case she usurped even more of my writing ops.

We moved away from each other like two antimagnetic forces. To me, she was like some proselytising monomaniac and, fittingly enough, I remembered reading an interview she gave where she'd talked of her parents being missionaries in India. I threaded my way over to a publisher, Niall, I used to go out with. There, I monologued brightly and loudly without listening to what he had to say. I couldn't concentrate any more as I was aware of this black spot on my horizon. Out of the corner of my eye, I watched Erin set down her glass on the table and leave. Her wine was untouched.

Back at home her words kept pinballing around inside my cranium. Perhaps I'd become too self-satisfied with my writing level. My only aspiration was to keep producing more of the same in the knowledge that some days my work transcended its limitations and other days it didn't. Murakami had recently shocked people by saying the best writing was done by under-forties. I was forty now and while I disagreed with him, I recognised that I'd replaced some of my youthful freshness with meticulous polish. But, and this is important, I believed in my genius. And though every passing year made it unlikely I'd exchange my Cork publisher for a big London one, I still thought I'd make it. Even so, perhaps Erin had a point; if I read more contemporary writers, I might learn the stylistic tricks to appeal to London publishers.

The worst thing about the conversation with Erin was it made me doubt myself. Doubt is absolutely terminal to a writer. Confidence is everything. If I was a Hemingway, Bukowski or a Colette I'd have told Erin to fuck right off. The fact I hadn't, proved I wasn't at the peak of my convictions. As a consequence, I fatally stepped back from my novel to reread and analyse it.

In the meantime, I kept an eye on Erin on social media. She was an inveterate oversharer and her following rose by the day. She had a knack of communicating, banal enough to connect with everyone, yet wry enough to set herself apart. Her shtick was to let the untalented think they could become great writers through hard work and practice. She was peddling the Erin Campbell University of Literature together with some kind of literary fashion blog. She hilariously selfied herself in her latest outsized sunglasses against shelves full of alphabetically ordered books. My own books were in collapsed piles on the floor – compared to Erin's bookcase, it was like the devastation of Bakhmut.

I couldn't help thinking of my favourite film, *All About Eve*, about a young actress who wheedles her way into the life of a doyenne in order to supplant her. With this in mind, I went back to Erin Campbell's story in the *Guardian*. I saw that she used a funkier idiolect than me, peppering her story with 'diss', 'emosh', 'rizz', 'based' and 'keeping it real', but I also detected a resemblance to my own style in her expression of erotic thoughts. I could tell she'd been studying me.

Erin Campbell, Erin Campbell, Erin Campbell. Is it any wonder the name has a ring to it when it includes the word 'bell'? Look, to be fair to her she wasn't the only person to plot a course straight to the top, but as soon as she was there, she wanted to dominate to a degree that none of us had a look-in while at the same time claiming to advocate on our behalf. After a literary conference, she tweeted:

> *I'm so inspired by the conversations and supportiveness within our amazing writing community. From now on, I'm going to tirelessly promote Northern Irish writers around the world any chance I get.*

She didn't. But, oh, the selflessness of the proclamation! The literary world swooned at her feet. All she did to promote others was write a complimentary tweet about someone's book in return for one on her own. It was transactional. Functional. When she gave interviews, I checked to see if she'd mentioned her peers. Not one of our names did she give. The irony was that she talked of being part of a rich tapestry of writers yet she was weaving her own legendary status. If she deigned to toss a name to the press, it was of a shining star in the literary firmament, an Enright or a Rooney to which she could hitch her personal luminescence.

I used X sparingly as a promotional tool. I didn't really get why I'd want fifty obsessive strangers commenting on my pronouncements. I'd no aspirations to be a cult leader, but Erin's example did encourage me to use X more to my benefit. I began to think to myself, ok, perhaps it's a good thing that Erin Campbell is shaking me up.

Of course, my real target should never have been Erin Campbell. It was the literary establishment at fault here and Erin was only a figurehead for their hypocrisy. When I complained to my publisher Marion, she replied severely, 'Erin Campbell's a celebrity now. She made the connections, so now she's reaping the rewards.' Marion's inference was that I should have spent more time cultivating friends myself and, though it pained me to admit it, she was right.

The second time I saw Erin Campbell was when we read together at Queen's. I'd always loved reading in the

Hogwartian wood-panelled Great Hall. Portraits of past dignitaries looked down snootily from the walls as we read – it was like being appraised by the great and the good and the dead. Erin Campbell's first short story collection had just been published by a London publisher to acclaim. She selfied us as we did our book-signing, but I didn't return the compliment as I rarely bothered with photos. We chatted a little. She told me a film company had bought the rights to her *Guardian*-winning story and I duly congratulated her.

'I've been meaning to ask you,' she said. 'What are the best subjects to write about right now?'

'An imagined war in the future,' I replied automatically. The very second I said it, I caught my breath, but it was too late. My idiotic honesty. I could see her narrow her eyes as she contemplated it.

'You mean like war spilling over from Ukraine?' she asked.

I'd let the cat out of the bag, so I thought I'd better come clean and own it, make sure she knew it was my territory. 'Yeah, I'm actually in the middle of a dystopian novel about Sino-Russian forces invading Northern Ireland. It captures those zeitgeist fears of the world disintegrating.'

'What a great idea.'

Her eyes flickered hectically as she thought it over. I'd stamped my ownership on the idea, but should never have revealed my secret. She wandered off to circulate, twirling a champagne glass prop in her hand. She was wearing a tight silver top accentuating the few curves she had, as she undulated her way through the crowd. Silver like the cold-blooded fish she was. I watched her for a while; some moments she was sexual as she turned on the charm, but mostly it was curious how sexless she seemed.

We ended up chatting together to a book festival curator. Erin was holding forth on her plan to start up a writers' commune.

'Yeah,' I chipped in. 'Maybe I could run a writers' bootcamp. Get them up at six am to write and breakfast withheld unless they reach a thousand words.'

The curator laughed, but Erin Campbell didn't appreciate the satire.

'You're a mentalist, you know that?' she said, staring icily at me.

I didn't mind being called a mentalist. It was better she assumed I was mad than outright hostile, but I should have played the game and said nothing. The last thing I wanted was for Erin Campbell to hate me. Especially as she was becoming an establishment gatekeeper. Later, I found myself standing with Niall in earshot of her talking about her movie deal.

'She's always bragging,' I whispered.

'Yeah, she's doing brilliantly,' said Niall, 'but she's going to have a hard time keeping that level up over the next years. There's no point in being jealous as one day her bubble will burst.'

Niall was in his fifties and had long since abandoned his dreams of making the big time. That was why he could afford to be kind to young talent. Unlike him, I would never abandon my ambitions. I'd keep them to eighty or ninety, however long it took – Christ, I'd even be trying to write a killer poem on my death bed. In the interim, if I had to be the Salieri to Erin Campbell's Mozart, standing in shadowy corners observing her bright light, then so be it.

The next month, my books were review-bombed on Amazon. There was no review per se, but they each received an anonymous one-star rating. It was impossible to tell who my nemesis was, but I did think back to Erin Campbell's deathly stare. Soon she was announced as judge of a notable award for short story collections. My latest collection, well-received though it was, didn't even make the longlist. Kiboshed. I wasn't surprised.

My publisher Marion phoned up, urging me to use Erin's star power.

'Why don't you ask Erin Campbell to endorse your novel?' asked Marion.

'Sure we don't like each other.'

'That may be, but she's playing a blinder. She's Erin Ní Cathmhaoil now.'

I looked up Erin's new gambit online. She'd gaelicised her name on Instagram. She knew the power of reinvention, of keeping people guessing.

Meanwhile, I kept working on my novel. I'd started reviewing for a bit of cash which slowed things down, but eventually I hit seventy thousand words and was days away from the editing process. I was so absorbed in it I rarely thought of anyone else and I was also deeply worried about money, as my landlord had decided to sell up. I had to move into a more expensive house, so I didn't know how I'd make rent. I kept having nightmares about being thrown out and having to sleep in some dorm in a writers' commune.

Finally, an opportunity came my way. It was an offer to go to Valencia and give a keynote speech for an academic conference on Northern Irish literature. I was thrilled and the news that Erin Campbell was the other speechmaker didn't bother me at all. I'd deliver a great talk and have a wonderful time.

Two days before my Valencia trip, the biblio-bombshell dropped. The nightmare. It was splashed over X that Erin Campbell's new dystopian novel was going to be released by Picador the following spring. I was horrified. I quickly read the premise – 'Set thirty years in the future on the eve of a new world war, this much-awaited debut is a searing examination of a teenager's life within an autocratic Irish state.'

I heard myself cry out again and again. My neighbours probably thought I was being murdered and in some way I was as Erin had ripped out my heart as a writer. In a panic, I phoned Marion and told her to look at Erin's latest post.

'Oh no!' she exclaimed.

'Can you still publish my novel?' I asked.

'Hmm. I think we might have to shelve it for a while. Just so we're not duplicating.'

I knew what that meant. Publication was cancelled.

'The fucking plagiarist stole my idea! Shouldn't I tell everyone what she's like?'

'No, you'll only do yourself harm,' said Marion. 'You were stupid in the first place to give her the idea. What were you thinking, Adele? Why do you make these silly mistakes? Surely you know the game by now.'

I felt like cracking my head against the wall. The perfidy! And yet I could say nothing in public as I'd only look bitter and vindictive. The hours of life I'd devoted to this book and now it was dead, just because I'd lost the run of my tongue. In my room, I kept playing Radiohead on a loop with its screaming lead guitars.

> You do it to yourself, you do
> And that's what really hurts
> You do it to yourself, just you
> You and no one else ...

The next night I just about managed to scrape myself off the floor to go to my friend Ronan's for a party. Ronan was an amazing guy. He was in his forties, ran a profitable computer firm and was also the wildest party animal I'd ever met. I arrived early to talk to him in private before he went up for the night in his personal moon rocket. I don't think he understood all the hopes and dreams I'd invested in the novel, but he was indignant at the breach of trust. He knew what it was like to build your own business only for competitors to make their move.

'You have to get even with her. Suffering like this will screw you up,' he said. 'She's a fucking backstabbing oxygen thief and deserves no sympathy at all. You discussed your intellectual property with her under the assumed understanding you had copyright. You could sue her in a court of law, but it'd be time-consuming, costly and you might lose.'

'I can't believe I'll be with her in Valencia tomorrow. What will I say to her?'

His face lit up. 'I've got it. You'll just say she did you wrong, then you'll quietly sabotage her talk.'

He unzipped his leather drugs pouch. It contained all sorts of illicit gear ranging from coloured ecstasy pills to powdered snortables. It was like a kid's treat bag of Smarties and sherberts. He lifted out a tiny phial like a perfume sampler. It was nearly empty.

'This is liquid LSD. One drop on your tongue is enough to box you out your skull for at least twelve hours. What time's her talk?'

'Eleven am.'

'Perfect. Take her out for a drink the night before to somewhere busy and pop in a drop. Before you know it, bang, she's out of the conference. She messes with your career, you mess with hers.'

'No. I can't.' It wasn't my style to hurt people. There were many times I could have said spiteful career-ruining things about writers and I'd nearly always held back.

'You'll regret it if you don't,' he shrugged. 'Sure she's a fucking fame-hound. If she was around in Jesus's time, she'd have kicked Jesus out the stable to get all the limelight.'

'And what if I get caught on camera?'

He laughed out loud. 'Firstly, pub cameras are grainy as hell. Make sure it's busy and you're not at the actual bar. Secondly, you're only giving her some acid, it's not like you're taking her back to your hotel room and raping her. Jesus, you're giving the woman a story here.'

It was true. I could just imagine her writing a cautionary tale about the experience.

'It's a funny image, I'll grant you that,' I admitted, 'but it's not for me.'

I went to get a beer from his fridge. No matter what, I wasn't going to let Erin Campbell spoil my night.

The following morning, I had the hangover from hell. Erin Campbell picked me up at midday to drive down to Dublin Airport. I was Anadined up, looking like I'd been pulled through a hedge backwards. She was perky, armoured with makeup, hair impeccably straightened. I could barely look at her, but she went straight in for the kill.

'Now, Adele, I'm sure you've seen the posts about my new book and you probably think I stole your idea, but I promise you it hasn't anything to do with Ukraine. I based it on Gaza. Completely my own slant.'

'But dystopian,' I protested. 'Set in the future, a new world war. You've stolen my thunder. My publisher has shelved my book.'

'Look, I'm sorry, but she's completely wrong to do that. There's plenty of room for variations on themes. You should stand up to her.'

'No, what I should really do is throw you off the plane.'

She took her eyes off the road to check if I was being serious. 'Adele, I could never replicate what you do. And besides, the Booker Prize winner from a couple of years ago wrote a dystopian novel. These concepts are in the ether.'

'If only I'd never told you.'

'I just hope we can stay civil throughout the week.'

'Well, I don't know about you, but I'm going to have a ball. I don't intend to ruin it for anyone.'

I nodded off and didn't wake up till we reached the airport car park. We ended up rushing through security. When I stuffed my liquids back into my handbag, I noticed something rolling around in its depths. It was the phial of LSD. Jesus fuck! That absolute mooncat Ronan must have slipped it into my bag at the party. Luckily for me, it was so small the scanner hadn't picked it up. That could have been me caught for possession of Class As. A reputation for drugs was the kiss of death in Irish literature. I recalled that Erin Campbell herself had snitched on a writer for having a ring of white powder round his nostril during a literary event.

The relief of getting away with it lightened my mood and I had to laugh at Erin with her giant shades like she was a welder's apprentice. On the plane, she whipped out a mock-up book she'd been sent.

'Don't you read?' she asked.

'No. I prefer to people-watch. Or daydream.'

'I don't have time for all that. I read about two hundred books a year.'

'Why so many?'

'To write about them, talk about them. It's our job, Adele.'

'No, you're wrong. It's our job to observe the human zoo.'

She disgruntledly went back to her book as if I was stealing her precious time. I now knew exactly what I was going to do.

It was a balmy twenty-five degrees on arrival in Valencia. Our Northern Irish clothes hung heavily on our skin.

'I feel like I've just walked in from the Antarctic,' joked Erin.

Her sunglasses were perched on the top of her head. She clearly thought they looked cool whereas I thought they looked like a pair of brown beetle eyes sprouting from her scalp. We got a taxi to the medieval city centre. The sun was lowering through the winding streets, casting long Gothic shadows as we passed the wooden doors of cathedral after cathedral, the sandstone turning the pale golden fawn of horchata in the fast-fading light. I could hear Spanish guitar music playing in the little nooked bars. I was already in love with this city.

'This is my twenty-fifth trip abroad this year,' Erin told me proudly.

Twenty-five trips, two hundred books: there was something wildly OCD in her list-making. Of course, all of us writers were a bit obsessive and I myself had a rampant case of misophonia, but there was obvious neurodivergence in her evolution. Eve – olution. We were back to *All about Eve* again.

At our hotel, we changed into lighter clothes and then google-mapped our way to a local restaurant where the conference delegates were meeting. Erin led the way of course, being better organised than I was. She was the type for whom spontaneity was having breakfast three minutes earlier than usual. At the restaurant everyone made a fuss of her. She was the literary star with her imminent Picador release. She looked particularly magnificent tonight, her long straight black hair defying the humidity, the low lighting warming her delicate skin, her red silky top underlining her elegance.

'Are you writing a novel?' one of the organisers, Carmen, asked me.

'Yes. Yes, I am.' A key of pain twisted in the centre my chest.

'I'm sure I'll devour it,' she said encouragingly.

The tapas arrived at the table. There were croquettes, deep-fried cheeses and pork ribs that big you could make three Eves out of them. Carmen took the seat between me and Erin. It felt good to be separated. I chatted to an academic, Marta, who sat opposite and drank a wine she recommended. A few raindrops fell on our table.

'Ah, you brought the rain with you,' said Marta, laughing.

'You call this rain?' said Erin. 'This stuff is twenty degrees. Back home, we'd shower in this.'

After the meal, Carmen suggested going for a drink. Erin ummed and ahed as she didn't drink alcohol and wanted to go over her keynote speech, but I could tell she wasn't keen on letting me bond alone with Carmen and Marta, so she agreed to come along. The skiff of rain had passed and we walked along cobblestones that lay out like slabs of *turrón*. Erin kept catching her heels in the cracks. I could see the tattoo coiling out over her collarbone.

'My new novel tunes into the zeitgeist by encapsulating our fears of global disintegration,' she was telling Marta and, whether she'd forgotten what I'd said to her or thought I couldn't hear, I felt the cut of every word.

We found ourselves in a square between the old city and new and headed towards a packed pub. According to Marta, it sold the best beer in town.

'Somewhere quieter?' suggested Carmen.

'No, this looks fantastic,' I said.

At the bar, the voices around us were raucous. I helped Carmen carry the drinks, making sure she was the one holding Erin's Coke as we weaved past customers. There were no tables free, so we set our drinks on a wooden shelf along the wall. It was there that I opened the phial. Of course, I had a moment of doubt, but my act felt bigger than me, tapping into all the plagiarism we writers had ever experienced. The others were looking around, trying to avoid being jostled, so I took the opportunity to insert the dropper into Erin's glass. Ronan had said only a drop, but in my haste I wasn't able to check the quantity. It might have been a drop or two. Perhaps less than a drop. I watched Erin take a sip and excused myself, braving the crowd again. I dropped the phial into the toilet bowl and flushed it away. My pulse was racing.

'I'm a bit hot,' said Marta when I returned. 'Fancy going outside?'

I was all for it as we had to push through even more hordes of people. We set our glasses on an outdoor table groaning with beers and wines and it couldn't have worked better if I'd planned it. Arms and hands were flying all around us. Scores of people could have spiked us and we would never have known.

I silently urged Erin to down her Coke before the symptoms kicked in and, just as I wished it, she took a long drink. In no time she seemed animated, her eyes wider than ever.

'I'm feeling a bit strange,' she said faintly.

'It's late,' said Carmen. 'You're probably tired from your journey.'

'No. The candle's pulsing ... weird.'

I presumed she'd never tried hallucinogenic drugs before. I remember being freaked out my first time and that was even after being warned of its effects.

'We'll get you a seat,' said Marta, taking her over to a wall.

Erin's eyes had begun to dart. She sat down jerkily, like a short-circuiting automaton. She was sweating profusely. Carmen dived into the bar to get some water while Marta took a Spanish fan out of her bag and wafted it over Erin.

'Do you see all the lights?' Erin muttered. 'Something's gone wrong with me.'

Marta started phoning for a taxi to the hospital. Out of the corner of my eye, I noticed a waiter pick up our glasses, shaking the ice cubes out and adding them to his stack which he carried back to the bar. Just then, Erin's head slumped forward and I caught her before she hit the ground. I could feel the heat off her, smell the panic pouring from her body, feel her clamminess on my hands. Marta made the call for an ambulance. It soon came, all flashing blue lights and ear-splitting siren. The drinkers fell quiet and crowded round as the paramedics saw to Erin and stretchered her into the ambulance. Carmen and Marta said they'd take care of her and told me to go back to the hotel. I watched them leave and began walking back. The copper tiles on a church tower reminded me of a snake skin. I got hopelessly lost in the circling streets. I'd never expected Erin to end up in hospital. I'd wanted to damage her career, not her body.

In the hotel, I could smell her on me. I licked her sweat off my palms, almost in ecstasy at what I'd done, crying huge tears of relief and disbelief. I fell into bed, moving my hands over my body to help me calm down. I decided not to get too angsty about it. My actions had cancelled Erin's keynote speech and anything other than that hadn't been my aim. I slipped into a sweet deep sleep.

The next morning, the news was all over the conference. Erin Campbell was in a coma and her parents were on their way over to see her. She'd had a suspected stroke.

'What happened last night?' people kept asking me.

'I don't know. Erin just fell ill and collapsed.'

'Terrible, isn't it?'

'Yeah, and she was on such a high about her new novel,' I said.

'So young too.'

'Almost unbelievable.'

Funnily enough, no one mentioned the word spiked, though I heard through Carmen that the doctors said she'd taken a large dose of lysergic acid. The following day, I visited the police station with Carmen and Marta. My heart was shunting against my ribs. I went into the interview room on my own and was asked brief questions by a rotund bearded policeman who seemed to be reading the questions off without understanding them.

'Did anyone offer you drugs when you were out?' he asked desultorily. 'Did Erin Campbell offer you any drugs? Did you observe anyone tampering with her drink in the bar?'

I answered no to every question without elaboration. It was on the tip of my tongue to say that writers sometimes experiment with drugs just to write a story, but I decided it was foolish to volunteer anything. He got to his feet and disinterestedly said goodbye.

I didn't visit Erin in hospital as her parents and sister were by her side. Although I made sympathetic noises when I had to, I had a wonderful time out drinking every night and making new connections. As the only Northern Irish writer at the conference, I was feted and fawned over. My keynote speech about the writer as an individual went down a storm. I left with invitations to Prague, Boston and Beijing, but still found time to compose a heartfelt tweet on X on how deeply sorry I was about Erin's stroke and coma. She would have done the same for me after all. I revelled in writing it as if Erin had written it herself. Imitation is the sincerest form of flattery. Imitation is the sincerest form of battery as well, as I was making sure if she recovered, that publishers and festivals would think her too ill to include in their schedules and choose me instead. I received over ten thousand likes, the most I'd received for any post.

At home on a friend's computer (I wasn't going to implicate myself by using my own), I did some research. 'Ischemic Stroke Secondary to Use of LSD' went one academic journal. I told myself that people had neurological reactions to all sorts of drugs.

'What the hell? Did you tip in the whole heap?' Ronan asked me when I saw him.

'Course I didn't. It might have been more than a drop though.'

'She probably never had a drug in her whole life and her body went into shock. But look, how were we meant to know she had an existing weakness?'

'True,' I said, eager for exoneration. 'Her writing schedule probably half-killed her. For all we know, the LSD was just a coincidence.'

The news came that Erin Campbell was being flown home in an air ambulance for more treatment. I wrote a moving piece for the *Irish Times* about what had happened that night in Valencia. I acknowledged the whispers about LSD in Erin's blood, but diplomatically said it was not for us to speculate on the circumstances. A few days later, Picador announced that they were postponing Erin Campbell's novel to 'a more appropriate time'. On seeing this, I immediately phoned Marion.

'Brilliant news,' she said. 'Let's go ahead with your novel. I'm sure yours will be a lot better than Erin Campbell's. She was the anointed one, but now *you're* the star.'

I began to be deluged with work. I travelled to eleven countries in the subsequent six months. I was on my way to New York when I saw on Facebook that Erin Campbell's life support had been switched off. She'd never regained consciousness.

I had to move fast before another writer feasted on Erin Campbell's fame. The vampires were everywhere in the writing world. I immediately set up a GoFundMe to establish a memorial in her name. I suggested a plaque and perhaps a bronze sculpture next to the Lagan where she used to walk every day and post photos of the occasional regal swan. 'What a marvellous idea, Adele,' the writers mewled. 'Many thanks for organising this, Adele. Erin would have loved this.' I hardly thought so. If Erin was up in heaven, she'd be spewing vile hatred at me, but I adopted the gravitas of an Arts and Culture Minister and replied:

> *It's times like these that the Northern Irish arts community must come together and celebrate the life of our greatest advocate.*

I said this for the benefit not of the writers, but the academics, the publishers and the arts administrators who would lap it up. Erin Campbell had taught me well. I'd always been an idealist hoping against hope that literature would be a meritocracy, but now I knew exactly how to behave. I had to be a social media construct in order to achieve my dreams. 'There is a splinter of ice in the heart of every writer,' Graham Greene once wrote, but in some of our hearts was a fucking avalanche. I found it deliciously ironic that Erin Campbell, who had been so anti-drugs in her lifetime, was now connected to drugs forever.

I went to the funeral, of course. I wore my black wool coat.

The best of us has left the stage. The rest of us must keep her flame alight, I tweeted with a crying face and fire emoji.

At home, a memory came back to me. When I was fourteen, I went with a friend to a house party. We crashed in the living room where an eighteen-year-old boy was lying pissed on a rug. I fell asleep in an armchair while my friend slept on the sofa, but later I woke up to see her letting the boy sneak in under her blanket. The blanket moved back and forth, they kissed, his breathing deepened. I listened and knew I should call him out, stop him from impregnating her, but I just couldn't for it was unbearably exciting and I longed to write about it in my diary. I froze and knew to my bones at that exact moment I was a born writer, a true writer, an explorer of life, an irresponsible voyeur of the depraved world.

But I never thought I'd kill someone. Not that I did. I just never imagined I'd take action against another writer. And it was somewhat painful to me that I'd never be able to write about it.

I was notified by a new email alert. It was an invitation to another trip – this time to Brazil. That made around twenty-five trips this year. To celebrate, I switched on 'Murder on the Dance Floor' full blast, tore my clothes off and danced naked along the landing of my newly-purchased house.

Brewboy East

Belfast was deeply uncool. That was Leon's first thought on his return from London. As he travelled in a taxi along the Newtownards Road, he took in the faded façade of the Conn Club and muted black livery of the Grand Eastern Bar and knew what he wanted to do. He'd been managing a tap room in London that pulled in customers like a magnetic vortex.

The taxi windows were beginning to steam up as if the rainclouds themselves were sneaking in by stealth.

'The weather's been far worse since Brexit,' quipped the taxi driver, 'cause we left all that sunshine behind in Europe.'

At the traffic lights, Leon noticed a tap room in an industrial building that would have depressed the life out of you. Further up the road, he almost laughed out loud at the sight of Horatio Todd's. What a horror show, he said to himself of its dun exterior – more like Sweeney Todd's! Its beer garden resembled a soulless barnyard with its black-barrel tables and Guinness awnings spattered with pigeon droppings.

He'd originally booked to come for his great aunt's ninetieth birthday party, and on hearing she was donating half of her savings to him to the tune of eighty grand, he'd decided to stay longer to scope out a business op. He'd never be able to invest in a Tottenham pub with that paltry sum, but in East Belfast it was more than possible. The lower part of the Newtownards Road was all bookies, bargain basements, and burnt-out businesses, but it was within spitting distance of the more gentrified areas.

The morning after his great aunt's shindig, he scoured the road again, drinking in the semi-derelict buildings. Revolution was on his mind, revitalisation, buzzwords that could form the perfect business plan. Over the next week, he plotted his future in his parents' house on Martinez Avenue, lined with leafy aspens, chestnuts and cypresses.

'Are you sure you shouldn't go back to London?' his mother asked, her worried eyes surveying him.

'No chance. I'm only a glorified pint-puller over there.'

It was worse than that. His girlfriend doctor of three months had just dumped him because of his job. She worked earlies at the hospital whereas he'd worked lates at the tap room. 'It's like we're in different time zones,' she'd said, crushing his heart. 'You're West Coast America, I'm Greenwich Mean Time. I never get to see you.' Dating her was like being in a long-distance relationship. He needed to take control, to be in charge of his own time.

He downloaded the forms for a start-up grant and found the perfect spot. It was a former factory workshop from the nineteenth century, built from brown bricks and hidden down a side street. There were intimate rooms he could transform into a quirkily nooked bar and enough space for a brewery. He walked out onto the Lower Newtownards Road and looked back at it. There was a palm shoot sprouting from its ramshackle chimney in the sun and it seemed a sign that something more exotic could flourish in these down-at-heel streets. He continued along the puddled pavements, his boots flattening the belly-up autumn leaves, and sized up the competition. Across the road was the Grand Eastern Bar and by its entrance was the cardboard cutout of a newspaper boy delivering news of the Titanic's demise. Trying to cash in on the tourist market, thought Leon, but a few cruise-ship Americans swinging by for the obligatory glass of Guinness was hardly going to boost the coffers.

A tall, dark-haired man swaggered out of the Grand Eastern to deposit two chairs on the pavement. He whistled in the way that people often did when the wind blew, as if imitating its power. He caught Leon's eye and gave a cursory nod. Leon nodded back, certain that the cockiness indicated ownership and left before the man had a chance to memorise his features. He already felt guilty about wanting to take the pub's business away.

'That area you're looking at,' warned his dad when he came home. 'You don't understand the complexities, the tensions, the feuds. It could swallow you up.'

'You're living in the past, Dad,' retorted Leon. 'The racketeers are on their way out.'

'It's still a big risk. All that cash invested and no guarantee.'

A wet leaf landed on the windowpane like a clammy hand spreadeagled against it. Leon's parents had never taken a risk in their lives. His mum had worked as a teacher till sixty, while his dad had been a conveyancing lawyer with a big firm. 'Keep your job till you get a better job,' had been his dad's advice to him as he was growing up, but his instincts had always shrieked against such conservatism.

That night, he couldn't sleep. It struck him he was taking the easy path by coming home. Was he just skinning out of London because he knew in his heart of hearts he couldn't make it there? London was the place to be if you belonged to an extended network of public-school alumni or immigrants; the truth was it was no place for anyone without family or connections. It was a graveyard for the lonely.

In the morning, he woke up to the sound of his mother's wire hangers cymballing in the bedroom next door. It sounded almost celebratory. The sky was propitiously sunny and when he looked across to the house opposite, a divaesque cat was occupying the centre stage of the window ledge, white blinds behind it like it was doing a curtain call. He checked his news feeds over a cup of coffee and, as luck would have it, he read about East Belfast being the hot spot for city breaks. It was the perfect time to call the estate agent and put in an offer. The building was owned by a business magnate called O'Doherty or O'Property as the locals called him, and the good news was it had been sitting on the market for months.

By the following afternoon, the offer was accepted. He made some phone calls to get building quotes and, as soon as he had the keys, set his renovations in motion. The plan was to install a secondhand microbrewery and open in the spring. He still had some savings in his account to start the revamp and he sent in applications for every grant on the go. He decided to christen his brewery and tap room Brewboy East as it sounded funky and hip.

At night, he could hear his parents talking in low troubled tones, trying to convince each other that the investment would pay off. His own array of doubts kept assaulting him, his eyes flicking open at five am. Dawn always came with a line of fiery clouds in the shape of tyre marks, denoting a world on the move. Even though he kept agonising over his spending, autumn was laying down its soft red carpet on the roads, encouraging him to stay the course.

It didn't take him long to install the fermenting vat. Everything was on schedule. One fuliginous December evening, he was locking up when he heard the Cranberries' 'In Your Head' pumping out from the Grand Eastern, a chorus of female voices singing the words at full blast. Outside the front door, a customer with a fag in his hand was complaining bitterly, 'Them lot are pissing me off rightly.'

Leon hopped into his van and pulled away. He tried to ignore the fact his neighbours, or rather rivals, were singing an anti-IRA anthem, showing their obsession with the past. He often had the feeling on the road that he was being watched.

He wasn't surprised when it finally happened. He'd just finished putting up the signage and was edging his way carefully down the ladder when a wiry man in his forties, his shoulders accentuated by a padded leather jacket, appeared.

'How's it going, son?'

'Getting there.' He suddenly felt unsteady on the ladder.

'Glenn from over-the-road's inviting you for a drink. He wants a friendly chat with you.'

Leon tried to affect a lightness. 'Great. I'm gasping. I've been meaning to call in for a while.'

It was three o'clock and the December sun was knocking off its own work for the day and disappearing beyond the mountains duveted with cloud and snow. He had more to do, but this was important. He stowed away the ladder and strolled over. The Grand Eastern was exactly as his friends had reported: red, white and blue bunting circumferencing the cornices of the high ceiling, the Guinness Time clock behind a brightly lit bar, the beermatted walls, the green leather upholstery and, most important of all, the Titanic memorabilia. The décor looked like it dated from the Troubles. A giant claymore was mounted on the wall.

Glenn stuck out a large hand between the pumps.

'Good to meet you, Leon. What'll it be?'

'A wee Jemmy then.'

'Oh. Prefer Irish to Scottish, do you?'

'I like both,' grinned Leon, trying to sidestep the politics.

He looked around him, taking in the edentulous old guys sitting at a table. Another ageing guy was coming out of the toilets, his right leg moving mechanically. Kneecapped in the Troubles, guessed Leon.

'On the house,' said Glenn, squirting Jameson's into the glass from the optic.

'That's good of you.'

'You won't feel that way in a sec ... I asked you here because your name is a problem for us. Brewboy East. We're the Grand Eastern. You can't just take over.'

'I'm not. It's a different market. Craft ale, I promise you, won't be stepping on your toes.'

'Change your name then. Two bars with east in the title a stone's throw away. It won't fly.'

Leon could feel the anger well up inside him. 'The East is not yours.'

'Oh, but it is.' Glenn was leaning forward with his two fists clenched on the bar. Muscles lined his forearms. 'We *are* the East. We *are* this street.'

Leon flung back his whiskey and got up from his bar stool. He passed a cardboard cutout of George Best in his Man Utd strip at the door and suppressed an urge to punch it in the face. The middle-aged man who'd fetched him was staring at him as he left. All he could sense was the silence. He crossed the road back to his building. There was a vibrating sensation in his chest. It wasn't as if he was even competing for the same custom. He didn't give a toss about the old man clientele of the Grand Eastern.

At home, he sat down to dinner with his mum and dad.

'Everything ok?' his dad asked, used to Leon's excited chatter at the table.

'Just a bit tired today.'

He didn't want to admit that his dad had been right with his warnings. Later that night, the words 'a stone's throw away' kept circling round his mind. Visions of smashed glass kept splintering through his dreams.

In the morning, under the bleached bones of cloud in the blue of the sky, he pulled down his signage. The Grand Eastern's shutters were closed but he knew they still saw him. He had to be magnanimous and let them have the copyright to the East. Perhaps East in the title was just a cliché after all. He'd name his tap room the Crafty Brew instead. There was nice irony in being crafty himself with the name change. He'd do anything to make his venture a success, even if it meant pandering to the Grand Eastern.

In March a new café opened on the road that sold spiced soya oatmeal lattes and almond milk cappos. It even sold açaí coffee although no one in Belfast could pronounce it. Leon rejoiced. If he knew anything, he knew the psychology of the middle-classes. They were happy to slum it if they felt they were in the happening area of town. Everyone loved the old made new. He was working hard, painting the walls, looking at potential web designs, setting up all the social media. He bottled his first batch of beer and it tasted perfect – crisp yet nutty. Not that he was in any danger of drinking the profits. Back in his teens, he'd been hit with so many hangovers he'd decided drinking was akin to striking a deal with the devil – four hours pleasure for twenty-four hours pain. Boozing was bad business on the body.

The morning of the Crafty Brew's grand opening, he was sitting on a paint-spattered bar stool, issuing last-minute invitations on his phone when the man in the leather jacket paid another visit. As Leon opened the door to him, a roll of thunder sounded and birds twitched on the eaves of a nearby roof before flying away.

'Looks good in here,' said the man with an admiring whistle.

'Six hours till we open,' said Leon.

'Yeah. Talking about that, Glenn would like another wee chat with you.'

The dread was dropping through him. 'Tell him to pop in any time.'

The man slowly shook his head. 'That's not how it works. He wants a serious chat.'

Leon stifled the desire to tell the man where to go, put on his coat and told the electrician he'd be back in twenty.

'Do you see this biblical weather?' said the man. 'Makes you think, doesn't it.'

The implication was that even God was against the Crafty Brew. The rain began to hammer down in steel-grey lines, rivets of water splashing off the tarmac. Instead of waiting for the traffic lights, Leon and the man made a dart for it through the cars.

'See that?' said the man, pointing out a derelict building with chipboard windows. 'That was the last time a bar tried to open round here. Must have been five years ago.'

'Times change,' replied Leon curtly.

The Grand Eastern was busier than before. This time, Leon noticed the portraits of George Best by local artists, but they were poorly executed. Almost as rudimentary as the Titanic mural on the gable end across the road. He couldn't help comparing them unfavourably to the surreal edgy paintings in the Crafty Brew.

'That's some day out there,' said Glenn in a friendly manner. 'A wee Jemmy for you?'

'Why not.'

A TV screen showed a muddy horse race somewhere in England, but the sound was on silent. A woman in a red cagoule came up to the bar.

'A Pepsi, please,' she ordered. 'No, wait – do you have low alcohol beer?'

'Do we fuck. What do you think this is, a holiday park?'

The patrons were highly amused. With every pint, they paid for a measure of banter. The woman who had a French accent emitted a nervous giggle. After Glenn had served her, he asked Leon to accompany him for a smoke. They stood in the porch as the rain pummelled down, the smell of damp on the old threadbare mat reminding Leon of wet dog.

'I might as well be open with you,' said Glenn. 'You're a problem for me.'

'Why?'

'You won't know this or want to know, but I was born in this pub. I don't want to lose it.'

'I don't want you to lose it either.' Leon tried his utmost to sound conciliatory. 'The more footfall on this road, the better for me.'

'You rich guys think you can just swan on in here, take over.'

'I'm not rich.'

'So, how come you've the cash to set it up?'

'Through the local council, government start-ups. There's big money to be had out there. You could get this place refitted yourself.'

'Really?' Glenn's eyes shone with interest in spite of his prickliness.

'Listen, I'll send you through the links in a couple of days.'

'But I'm not good with forms and writing and that.'

'Then ask me if you need some help. And you should come to my opening tonight. The investors will all be there.'

'Right, cheers,' said Glenn. 'I'll dander across alright.'

Leon belted down his whiskey, noticing the silver threads in Glenn's black hair and crinkles round his eyes like time was being stitched into his body. He'd been born in this pub and would die here.

'Better get back.' Leon handed Glenn his glass. 'Got a lot to do.'

'Better get back myself.'

As Leon crossed the road, he felt himself illuminated in a blink of yellow sheet lightning. More lightning came in rapid flickering succession like he was being papped by the press. He couldn't help thinking he'd won. It looked like he was being generous in passing on the forms and supporting a rival, but he instinctively knew Glenn wouldn't have the patience or mindset to fill them in. How could an old-school loyalist ever understand the etiquette of the funding game?

By six pm, Leon had chalked every last craft beer onto the menu board and made sure the artwork was hanging straight on the white walls. Under the exposed beams, the tap room felt like it was crossing cultures, hyperglobal yet local. There were three long tables and benches in bierkeller style as well as some comfier chairs in the nooks. European-Belfast, he designated the vibe.

'You did it!' his dad said, shaking his hand. 'I had my doubts, I have to say.'

'So did I,' admitted Leon with a smile.

'I'm just so relieved you've had no trouble. The Newtownards Road is much more progressive than I thought.'

He felt his dad's eyes rove over his, but he feigned a need to greet a guest and hurried away. Once the business was up and running, he would come clean about Glenn.

The next hours were a whirl of posing for press photos, greeting investors and charming potential customers. When the guests finally thinned out, he went out onto the road to wave his parents on their way. He wasn't surprised in the end that Glenn hadn't paid a visit. This wasn't Glenn's world, this modern tap room with defiantly crystal-clear windows and bright lights. Glenn wasn't the type to network; he insisted on people coming to him.

In front of him, Leon could see the Grand Eastern as black as the sky, the frosted glass preventing anyone from looking inside. The porch reminded him of a sentry box. These streets would always be watchful and secretive and he'd never fully belong. One day, Glenn might decide he'd had enough of him and order a visit by a few teenagers with rags in bottles. It was hard to live beside the past in this city.

Under the porch, there was the suggestion of a shadow and the faintest circle of smouldering orange, pulsating like a star. He could almost smell the cigarette smoke. He quickly turned on his heel, making a beeline for his own bright lights.

Acknowledgements

A huge thank you to my publisher Alan Hayes for providing me with the constant impetus to write, and to Damian Smyth from the Arts Council of Northern Ireland for the ongoing financial and moral support. Cheers to Patrick Fitzsimons for his painting of the Lagan Weir Footbridge. Immense thanks to Nora Hickey M'Sichili for the residency at the Centre Culturel Irlandais and to Maria Gaviña Costero for inviting me to the University of Valencia.

Thanks to Tanya Farrelly and Dedalus Ireland for publishing 'The Whistleblower', 'The Peacemaker' and 'Sexploits of a Rooftopper' in the *Take Six: Six Irish Women Writers* anthology, 2025.

Thanks to copyright holders for text from 'Sheela-Na-Gig' by PJ Harvey and for text from 'Just' by Radiohead.

About the Author

Argyll Images/Photography by Bernie McAllister

Rosemary Jenkinson is a playwright, poet and fiction writer from Belfast. She taught English in Greece, France, the Czech Republic and Poland before returning to Belfast in 2002. Her plays include *The Bonefire* (Stewart Parker BBC Radio Award), *Planet Belfast*, *Here Comes the Night*, *Michelle and Arlene*, *May the Road Rise Up* and *Lives in Translation*. Her plays have been performed in Dublin, London, Edinburgh, Brussels, New York and Washington DC. Arlen House publish her plays, *Billy Boy* (2022) and *Silent Trade* (2023), with *Manichea*, her play about censorship in publishing, forthcoming.

In 2018 she received a Major Artist Award from the Arts Council of Northern Ireland. She has been writer-in-residence at the Lyric Theatre Belfast, the Leuven Centre for Irish Studies and the Irish Cultural Centre in Paris. Her short story collections include *Contemporary Problems Nos. 53 & 54*, *Aphrodite's Kiss*, *Catholic Boy* (shortlisted for the EU Prize for Literature), *Lifestyle Choice 10mgs* (shortlisted for the Edge Hill Short Story Prize), *Marching Season* and *Love in the Time of Chaos* (shortlisted for the Edge Hill Short Story Prize). Her debut poetry collection, *Sandy Row Riots,* was published in 2024, followed by a debut novel, *The Memorisers*, in 2025. She is currently Royal Literary Fund Fellow at Queen's University.

The Irish Times has praised her for 'an elegant wit, terrific characterisation and an absolute sense of her own particular Belfast'.